THE CASTLE OF GIANTS

By the same author

THE ECHOING CLIFFS

Hjalmar Thesen

THE CASTLE OF GIANTS

With decorations by Elizabeth Lord

HUTCHINSON OF LONDON

HUTCHINSON & CO (*Publishers*) LTD
178–202 Great Portland Street, London W1

London Melbourne Sydney Auckland
Bombay Toronto Johannesburg New York

First published 1969

© Hjalmar Thesen 1969

*This book has been set in Bembo, printed in Great Britain
on Antique Wove paper by Anchor Press, and
bound by Wm. Brendon, both of Tiptree, Essex*

09 095800 4

For Guy, Christopher and Georgina

AUTHOR'S NOTE

Southern Africa in the seventeenth century was a vast, unexplored land of fabled riches, occupied by nomad Hottentots and Bushmen and teeming with game animals such as no white hunter had ever dreamed of.

In 1652 the Dutch East India Company, badly in need of a refreshment station for its scurvy-ridden ships, established a stronghold at the Cape of Good Hope. Jan van Riebeeck, the first commander and founder of present-day Cape Town, lost no time in building a protective fortress and in setting about his tasks of gardening and cattle trading with the mercurial Hottentots. But the interior beckoned constantly and the arrival of each new tribe with cattle to sell brought fresh rumours of gold and ivory.

A land of unending dreams and surprises, but of all the strange things, perhaps it was the men from Europe themselves who were the strangest.

I

'He was not always as you see him now.' The smoke
from the fire writhed upwards into darkness and the
woman turned her head away, covering her eyes with
her hand; her sentence hung unanswered and unchallenged in the cold air but the listeners moved in discomfort and one poked the fire with a stick, sending a
streamer of sparks towards the stars.

Far off, a jackal howled and a flush of light to the east,
across the sand flats, pointed to the rising of a full moon.
The woman cradled a tin cup in both hands and as the

moon began to spread its purple across the dunes, her eyes shone with a wild brilliance, for she was drugged with the dagga she had smoked. She sipped from the cup of brandy. 'He was not as you see him now.'

The woman wore a tattered skirt and her shoulders were covered by a thin shawl. Her breasts protruded uncovered and they were shapely full, curved and pointed with youth. A necklace of white beads hung down between them and rested on the skirt where it was stretched tight between her knees. The scarf tied about her head was a single point of alien colour by the red and black of the fire. The hypnotic sea droned in splendour and from beyond, where the lights of the fort began, there came the needle point of a violin. The night cast its spell and the woman's voice became the sound of the surf and the lilt of the violin and the weeping of the jackal. She tilted her head sideways, showing the long line of her neck and the high, delicate cheekbones; her lips were drawn sharp against the glowing heap of coals.

'Once he was strong. He was a good runner. He killed many animals. All he killed with his spears and his arrows. He was good. He was a strong man.'

She was no longer talking; her voice had risen to a high wailing note, a monotonous song beginning and ending with the same words, repeated over and over, rising and falling on the deep contrapuntal chorus of the still watchers. They echoed her, and the rumbling of their voices was like the sound of the sea when the wind flutes in indecision.

On the outermost rim of firelight, Harib leaned unmoving against the branch of a small, twisted tree, listening intently and his ears strained to hear each syllable while his lips moved soundlessly. Firelight ran red on his naked legs and arms so that the polished ivory bangles winked with it and the long muscles flowed deep with shadow. His face was impassive, but the upward tilt of his chin and the tensing and relaxing of his jaw muscles told of an emotion and a remembering.

The dead man lay close to the fire on a kaross of sheepskins so that the yellow of his skin and the jet black of his tight hair cap were intensified by the yellow light; stark too were the weals around his ankles where the manacles had rubbed and it was on these that Harib's eyes were fixed. But his mind was elsewhere; 'He was brave when the elephant ran among the hunters.' The woman sang and Harib remembered; he could hear again the squealing trumpet; how the ground had shaken, how the dust had swirled. 'He it was who killed the lion.' The lion; that had been a day. And the spear had gone into the lion's mouth and down into its heart as it sprang. It was a long time ago, but Harib remembered every detail, for it had been his first hunt; a boy carrying a man's weapons and hunting for the first time with the men.

The moon had risen clear of the hills and some of the people around the fire had stood and begun to dance, in a slow rhythm of mourning for the dead. Harib turned away. Behind him the singing mounted up on the moonlight, but the violin had stopped its keening and there was no sound from the fort. The fort lay purple and grey and silver under the night's radiance, a squat alien thing with its sloping, bastioned corners and its central tower; a thing of power with no need for a voice, only the menacing silence of its black cannon, like burnt trees angling across the skyline. Harib gripped his spear tightly, feeling a powerful emotion which was new to

3

him and unpleasant. It was not the sight of the dead man
which affected him so much; the man had been gone for
over a year, long enough to be blurred to reality and as
good as dead. It was the marks of the chain which made
his death seem grotesque and the hole in his shoulder and
the need for a brave hunter to crawl away like a wounded
animal and die alone. Harib's memory of the dead man
was coloured with hero-worship from his youth, but he
felt a kind of awe for those who could catch and eventually kill, so unconcernedly it seemed, so mighty a man.
Tomorrow he would see these strange white giants for
the first time, and he was both afraid and excited.

It began to rain during the night and when morning
came a misty rain was still falling. Harib with six others
stood dejectedly under the shelter of a scrawny tree,
warming themselves in the smoke of a fire and waiting.
The leader of the party looked very grand, Harib
thought, in his soft coat of which the two sides could be
held together by little pieces of round bone. The coat
hung down to the old man's knees and had a fringe of
hair, like stringy bark, around the lower edge. It was
black and had a blue patch worked in at the back. Harib
thought it a pity that such a garment should be getting
wet in the rain. His own sheepskin cloak was warm
enough, though, and it was waterproof; he also had a
pointed skin cap to keep the rain off his head and most of
the others were dressed in the same way, except the old
man's brother, who had heavy skin coverings on his feet
and black coverings on each leg like a cloak wound
round his waist and parted in the middle between the legs.
At the bottom this garment seemed torn. It was the same
colour as the old man's coat. The two elders, both grey-
bearded and wizened, desiccated rather, with age, like

4

over-dried skins, seemed quite willing to listen to any ideas as to what should be said at the meeting.

The rain stopped suddenly and a bright shaft of sunlight lit the towering blue wall of the mountain that leaned over them. They squatted around the fire and ate from a wooden bowl of thick milk mixed with some small pieces of dried fish. Beyond them lay the fort with its cannon gleaming wet in the sun; it seemed smaller in the daylight but more solid and dangerous; only the superstitious dread of the night was gone to leave tall, grey, unscalable walls and the watchtower like a chamelion's eye, peering down from every angle.

Harib listened but took little part in the discussion. His home was far to the east over the mountains and down in the lowland plains by the sea, a journey of many days. He knew nothing of the quarrel that these people had with the white giants of the fort except what he had been told. They had told him many things in the three days he had camped with them; he blessed his luck for having fallen in with these new companions and to be under the protection of their little white flag. Alone he would have been sadly handicapped and very likely killed, for he could not have known that a war of some sort was in progress.

The dead hunter had been the first of his tribe to journey westwards. He and his woman had gone away into the setting sun and they had never come back. The months had passed and legends grew. Strange vessels upon the sea had drifted slowly by on their white wings and rumours from the west had fired Harib's curiosity until he could rest no longer. His people had watched him go with the sort of reverence they accorded only to the very brave or to those who would soon die. And now he was in the land of the giants. He was about to enter the great

5

house where they lived. Their great sea things lay at rest in the bay without feathers, larger than he had ever imagined. And it was true that Kara had been killed by them. And Tara, his woman, was she mad? Harib found it impossible to concentrate for long on the harangue that still took place around him. His companions, he thought, were brave even to be so unconcerned by their imminent entry into the great house. True, they had met the giants, and even seen their women, and their leader had been into the house itself, but the interminable discussion about cattle grazing made him impatient; he was avid for more details of the terrible weapons which made smoke and fire and of the sea things and of the homes inside the great one. The wound in the dead man's shoulder had puzzled him. It was not the mark of a spear; they said it had been caused by the bright, heavy club which made smoke and fire. How could such a thing make a small round hole without the marks of fire?

Something was moving along the top of the fort and Harib called quickly in excitement, pointing, for the others had been deep in conversation. It would be one of them, he thought. He kept his eyes fixed to the top of the wall and watched in fascination as the mysteriously lifeless fort began to stir. A herd of cattle moved slowly away from it and his eyes jumped quickly, for three of the giants walked with the animals and they carried the clubs over their shoulders. Then four more began to go down the white road that led to the sea and he watched them all the way to the black structure that was built out into the sea of the bay. Now there came a long fluting sound not unlike the bellow of an ox and a coloured thing crawled up the stick mast to break fluttering gently

6

in the early morning breeze. But the smaller white houses near the great one remained silent and lifeless and Harib remembered that the giants and the water people, and the fish people too, were at war. He was struck with astonishment that these, who were the same as he was, with the same weapons, could have made the giants fear them. But the elders said so; they said that the little house giants and the garden giants had all gone into the great house for protection. Harib was deeply puzzled. They cannot run fast, the elders explained, their clubs are too heavy and they have heavy coverings on their feet. When they smoke and fire at us we run so that the stones that are thrown cannot hit us, so we come any time we wish into the gardens they have made and around the small houses. But they guard their cattle now, for the Cape men have stolen many.

'Have you killed any of them?' Harib asked.

'Some have been killed,' they said. A silence fell over the group.

'Why?' Harib asked.

'Because they fight with us,' the leader said at length.

'But why do they fight with you?'

The leader said patiently, 'Because the Cape men steal their cattle.' Then he added, 'This land they have taken from us.' He swept his arm across the horizon. 'They have bought many cattle and they have taken our land for grazing.'

Harib thought about this. He presumed the giants lived on cattle, which thought seemed to fit the picture he had in his mind, but he was still anxious. After a while he asked, 'Why did the giants come here, from where did they come?'

'They came across the sea,' the elder said, 'in their

"skippe", those in the water.' He indicated the ships with his chin. Harib looked absently across the bay to the open void of water beyond.

'But there is no land,' he said persistently. 'Do they live always in those until they come to find cattle?'

Now a great discussion began to take place. While the leader insisted that they came from a land across the sea (they had said so themselves) the others said, 'Which land, we can see no land.'

'It is too far away to see,' the leader insisted.

'Surely such a land would have mountains which one could see no matter how far away it was.'

'You cannot see the mountains of the Cape from the Namaqua country,' the leader argued.

'Yes, but there are too many other mountains in the way,' they said. 'Here is the open sea, there are no mountains to hide anything.'

The leader was getting angry. He changed the subject slightly. 'They came from a land across the sea to trade for cattle,' he said with finality.

The others were all on Harib's side now. 'Have they no cattle in their own country? Why do they not drink the milk as we do and let the cattle increase? Why do the skippe sail off to the east sometimes? How did they learn to eat cattle if they lived always on the sea?' The discussion had degenerated into individual arguments and the leader looked relieved that the main attack was off him. Harib turned to him.

'Surely they cannot live in that big house for ever?'

The old man shrugged his shoulders. 'When they first came,' he said, 'we traded with them, thinking that they would soon go away and they gave us many strange things in exchange for our cattle. They then built the big

8

house and still we traded with them, for they did us no harm. Now they have many cattle and we have few and they use our grazing grounds and now we wish that they would be gone.'

Harib looked again towards the fort from which a trickle of smoke was coiling up into the sky and this at least he thought was less mysterious; the sight of the cattle, too, had been comforting. Now it seemed that three figures were coming out of the entrance of the big house towards them. As they drew closer, the discussion ceased, and all eyes turned in their direction.

The three giants, for such they undoubtedly were, wore a wonderfully rich and strange variety of garments and ornaments. They also carried fire clubs and long thin sticks in their belts and bandoliers from which bright objects dangled. They were clothed in garments not unlike those that the elder and his brother wore and they had heavy coverings on their feet. Their legs seemed painted black, but one had white painted legs and they all had wide coverings on their heads like black mushrooms. The faces of two of them Harib saw were partially covered with hair and the skins of their faces were very white and pink, like the undersides of young mushrooms. They were tall, but these surely could not be the giants; these were men, not real people like himself and his companions, Harib thought, but they were men nevertheless. He came to the conclusion that they were the slaves of the giants, the sourijs he had heard of, who looked after the cattle and fought with fire clubs and sticks. The sourijs beckoned and they followed in silence.

As they drew near to the great house, Harib began to feel a quickening of excitement. The walls towered higher and higher and the gate which leaned open to

9

receive them could have admitted many cattle abreast. Harib looked about him wide-eyed. This was the most wonderful structure he had ever seen. He felt as though he were in a canyon with sheer walls in which there were many holes and he knew that he was trapped and at the mercy of he knew not what. The sourij people seemed to be everywhere. They stood, some of them, high up on the top of the walls and others looked out from holes. He was almost blinded by the colours they wore; they were like flowers in the veld after rain and their clubs and sticks shone when the sun rays caught them and became dazzling like white stone.

The three sourijs were going up a thing made of wood which took them towards a large dark hole and Harib followed his companions gingerly. Now they were in a dark hut made of wood full of heavy wooden ornaments upon which other sourijs sat, but with their feet upon the floor; and on the floor was a soft covering of many colours, but it was not made of skin or grass. Harib felt it with his hand. The three sourijs sat on the floor and beckoned the real people to do likewise, so they all sat and looked up at other sourijs who sat on the high things. In the centre of the hut was another large wooden thing with a flat top upon which many strange objects lay. Some of the sourijs sat close by the big thing so that they could rest their hands upon it. Harib saw that most of them had taken off their head coverings, and he was amazed to see that their hair was of many different colours and that it was so long that it hung upon their shoulders. One of them had hair that was the colour of bitou bush flowers.

As his eyes became accustomed to the gloom, he saw that the hut in which they sat was more of a cave with a flat ceiling and flat walls, upon which there leaned and hung a new unfolding of shapes, some shining as the surface of water and some dark and smooth as black stone. Still more sourijs were entering and to Harib, looking up at them from his cross-legged seat on the floor, they did indeed loom over him and his companions like giants.

A strange muttering came from all sides like wind beginning to stir in a forest and even the smell was different from anything Harib had ever known; the smell of leather he knew and could detect but the overwhelming musk-like pungency of other odours almost suffocated him. The sourijs were nearly as tall as the doorway through which they came, no giant could enter here; were these then the giants themselves or did the giants live in another part of the great house? As he pondered, wide-eyed, a tiny figure came forward into the centre and stood still, while the sound of voices began to fade away. With surprise Harib saw that this was a woman, covered from head to foot in a long coloured garment, but he could see that her feet were bare and that she was a real person like himself. The sourij in the black garment with the white face and the black hair that lay on his shoulders and the line of hair below his nose was speaking in a tongue that was slow and ponderous, like the far-off sound of the sea, and there was silence as he spoke. When he had finished the woman turned and said to Harib and the others on the floor, 'The lord from over the sea bids you welcome and says that he only desires peace and friendship with the real people.' To hear his own language under such circumstances seemed unnatural. The woman continued, 'Let your leader speak now and the lord and his men will listen.'

The elder licked his lips and began; he looked directly

at the woman. 'Tell the sourij lord that we bring greetings and come in peace, for we are weary of bloodshed and are anxious to return to our old grazing grounds.'

They waited while the low speech flowed on again. Presently the woman turned. 'The sourij lord says that you can come back and he will be pleased to make peace, but first you must return all the cattle that have been stolen.'

The elder and his brother shifted and looked at each other and then held a huddled conversation which Harib could not catch. 'We know nothing of the stolen cattle,' he said at last, 'the Gorachoquas stole the cattle and they have gone away to the north.'

Harib heard the chief sourij sigh heavily before turning to speak to the woman. 'The sourij lord says that your people may come back but that they must first go and journey to the north and find others who have cattle to trade and bring them here and if many cattle come then you will be well rewarded. Also you must not harm any of the sourij people or steal from them, otherwise the peace will be at an end.'

'It is good,' the elder said, 'we will try. There are rich tribes in the north. If the Cochoquas come you will not see the grass for their cattle.' The sourij lord looked from the woman to the elder and then spoke to the others who sat near him. He seemed interested, even excited. The elder looked at the others with obvious pride. He said again, waving his arm in emphasis and with a boastful tone, 'They will eat up the grass like locusts and you will not have enough copper and tobacco to buy even a small corner of them.' Once more the voice from the table rumbled.

'The sourij chief is very pleased to hear this,' the

12

woman said, 'You will be well rewarded if you can cause the Cochoquas to come here.' A voice from the table interrupted her. 'Cochoquas,' she said again distinctly, looking at the sourijs. One of them, Harib noticed, was peering intently at a white square thing before him upon which he seemed to be drawing with a feather.

'The sourij chief says many more ships will come with copper and cloth and beads and tobacco and that there will be enough to buy many cattle.' She paused to listen, turning her head and half leaning in concentration. Then she stretched out her hand to take the thing which the sourij chief had removed from his finger.

'The chief asks whether the Cochoquas of whom you speak have any ornaments like this,' and she passed the ring to the elder. The old man looked at it and Harib craned forward to see the little circle of yellow. He felt it and it was smooth and heavy; it was made of the same stuff as the pendant of his necklace. He lifted the chunk at the end of the thong to make certain and as he did so the sudden sound before him caused him to look up. The sourij chief was standing and gazing at him, others peered over his shoulder. Slowly the chief sat and turning, spoke to the woman; there was a murmuring in the hut. The woman held out her hand saying, 'The chief would like to see your necklace.' Harib glanced at his companions and saw only blank faces so he pulled the thong over his head and handed it to her.

The sourijs crowded round their chief and they sounded excited or angry, Harib could not tell which. Slowly the tangle of great hands and heads and shoulders moved away to reveal the sourij chief and in his hand the necklace with its heavy yellow stone; slowly he rubbed the stone up and down between his fingers, but it was already so smooth from the friction of Harib's chest that it could gleam no more than it did. Harib wanted to tell him this, but he was afraid to speak. The sourij was looking at him and smiling. The woman said, 'The sourij chief wishes to know where you got this heavy stone and whether you have more for trade.' A shiny box was being opened on the floor behind her and from it flowed an assortment of coloured and strangely shaped things. Harib looked from the box to the woman, not fully comprehending; he was conscious of many eyes upon him and upon his necklace which was being passed from one hand to another. The woman had spoken of trade. If they wanted to trade something for the necklace, Harib felt that he would be obliged to co-operate if only for the sake of the real people who had befriended him. But he was not keen to part with it. He wanted to tell them that it could not bring them luck for it was his personal talisman. Could they not see its shape? An eland cow reclining in sleep? He would not have kept it otherwise. As for more, well, they could see he only had the one.

The woman spoke to him, but this time her voice was not loud and official. 'Whence do you come, hunter man?' she asked softly.

Harib looked around him, as though searching for the sun. 'From the sunrise, many days' journey from here.' Then he added, 'I am of the Outanqua people.'

'Are there many such stones in your country?'

'Many,' he said. 'In the streams there are many but not of the same shape.'

The woman said reflectively, 'Outanqua, was not this Kara of your people?'

'He was Outanqua, yes.'

There was a small silence between them, but it passed unnoticed, for Harib's companions were chattering and reaching for the shiny cups that the sourijs were handing out.

'The sourijs will trade many things for such yellow stones,' the woman said.

Harib took the cup that was offered to him and looked at it in admiration. It was smooth and shiny and symmetrical. This was certainly the most wonderful thing he had seen so far in the house, of the sourijs. A really useful thing of great beauty; he fondled it, wondering how it was made and of what, then he looked at the amber-coloured liquid inside and sniffed it. He tasted it and then drank some as the others were doing. It burned his mouth and his insides felt hot as fire; he coughed and wiped his eyes which had misted with tears. But this is honey drink, he thought, only much stronger, very strong, very good. He turned to the leader who had finished his cup and was wiping his lips. 'This is like the honey drink we make in the forests in my country.' He was excited to find that there was something he had in common with the utterly alien sourijs. But the leader was having his cup refilled and seemed to have lost interest in anything else. Harib drained his and they filled it again at once. He could not understand how the necklace had suddenly made him the centre of attraction, but eyes were upon him he knew; he could feel it and see the faces over the rim of the cup as he drank. Heads were craning from the back to see him over the shoulders of the towering sourijs, and strange bright things were being spread out in front of him on the floor.

Vaguely he wondered whether his eland hunting charm could have any connection with the giants' desire for cattle and the luck it might bring them, but somehow it seemed unlikely. He looked at the assortment of treasures growing in a heap on the floor. Much of the soft garment stuff was visible in an endless variety of colours; he felt it and sniffed it, but he was not over-excited by it. It would be too thin to keep out the cold, he thought, and far too bright to hunt in. The bead necklaces were wonderfully intricate and bright and the heavy red bracelets also pleased him, but the cup remained the most wonderful of all and it seemed to be growing brighter. The sourij chief was still watching him, but he was no longer nervous of the piercing eyes. A roaring of voices seemed to be growing in his head and the faces before him waved and swam in a mist of dark and light. The woman was speaking, but he could hardly hear her voice, and then slowly the hut began to revolve about him in a blinding maze of colour and sound until he no longer knew nor cared whether he was sitting or dancing or floating away.

2

Harib awoke to a pounding headache and waves of nausea which seemed to pour down upon him from a single hole of light far above him. He lay for only a second after opening his eyes and sat up so quickly that his head was pierced twice through with pain and his heart beat almost audibly in the dim silence. He found that he was lying on a pile of the soft garment stuff and when his eyes could focus and adjust themselves he saw that he was in another square hut made of wood. He thought for a time that it was the same one he had been in before, but in pondering and remembering he found that it was smaller. A wooden platform for sitting on and another larger flat one for putting things on stood in the centre of the hut.

He swayed to his feet and inspected the four walls closely, but the wood rapped solidly under his knuckles and he could find no way to get out. He sat down on the sitting platform in a half-conscious experiment and then noticed for the first time that on the higher platform was an earthenware pitcher which he found contained water, and, beside it, a round, hungry-smelling brownish object the size of a small rock rabbit. He drank nearly half the pitcher of water and then picked up the brown loaf and smelled it again. He nibbled the end of it and found it good to eat, quite unlike anything he had ever tasted before, but bland and satisfying, reminiscent of a burnt mushroom.

As his headache faded, its void was filled by ever clearer memories of the meeting with the giants and the sudden turn of events his necklace had precipitated. A quick glance told him that the charm was once again in its place around his neck and this surprised him, for he knew that they wanted it. He lifted it and weighed it in his hand with a puzzled expression; not every stream contained the heavy yellow pebbles, but in the black water, far away where tall forests sprawled under the mountains and gravel beds glowed yellow as honey in the noon sun, where the river bank was cut deep by the tramping of elephants and buffalo, where he and Kara had hunted and gathered honey, here the stones lay; here in the silence of the great forest, in the green and golden silence that was broken only by the sound of trickling water or the peal of a bird.

Clearly in his imagination he could see it and he felt pleasure in remembering. Not all the pebbles were as big as this, the size of a rock pigeon's egg, but there were many; he wondered whether they would want smaller ones too. Then he began to doubt his assessment of the morning's events; he had misunderstood so much of what had happened and the entire episode was so like a dream that he could not trust his judgment now. But the imprisoning walls were real and he knew that he was inside the awesome house of the giants. Curiously, he felt little fear, only a great interest to see again the towering white-faced people and the curious, pretty things they possessed, for they were obviously great possessors. Above all, he wanted to see the weapons with which they could make smoke and fire and with which they could kill. For the time, Harib was content to wait; there was nothing he could do.

As the beam of light from the single high window shifted, so he guessed the passing of time. He was asleep when new light flooded in upon him and he sat up to see the woman before him suddenly in a high square of brilliant daylight. He got quickly to his feet, pleased and excited. He had no doubt it was the same woman who had been the interpreter, for he had never seen a woman of his own kind dressed as she was. Then he saw her face and she was smiling at him. 'Are you awake now?' she said. 'Did you drink too much?' She shook her head and clucked with her tongue as though talking to a child, but Harib could see that she was laughing.

'Woman,' he said, 'this is very strong drink, too strong. Are the bees then also as big as these sourijs in this country?'

The woman giggled and walked into the room as

Harib scratched his head self-consciously. She picked up the half-eaten loaf and took a bite, looking around her as she munched.

'Why did you come here?' she asked.

Harib glanced at her and then walked into the sunlight of the open doorway. A wooden ladder led down, far down it seemed, to the ground and at the foot of it stood a sourij giant with a club. Harib blinked his eyes and looked again; surely there was a trickle of blue smoke coming from the thing? He stepped quickly back and then peered out again. On his right was a sheer wall of wood. In front there was the ladder and the sourij with the smoking club. Beyond him was a vast open space with a single sourij walking slowly across it, and, beyond, the wall of the great house rose steeply up to obscure everything and to cast a dark shadow that leaned towards him. He turned to the woman and could no more think of smiling.

'We had seen the skippe,' he said.

The answer seemed to satisfy her, for she nodded and took another bite of the loaf. She turned and held out her hand. 'Let me see your necklace,' she said. Harib gave it to her. She examined it closely.

'It is my hunting fetish,' he said, almost in apology. 'See that fold there and this one, it is like an eland asleep.'

'It is pretty,' the woman said, handing the necklace back; 'the sourijs will trade many fine things for such heavy stones. They wish to be friends with you and your people. Would you like to see some of the things they can trade?'

'Why did they kill Kara?' Harib asked.

The woman sat down and nibbled at the loaf with

white even teeth. 'It was a mistake,' she said, 'and the sourijs are sorry. He ran away and they killed him with their fire weapons, but they did not mean to.'

'He ran away,' Harib said mockingly, swinging on his heel, then he turned upon the woman. 'Kara would only escape, he would not run away. Why was he a prisoner? He was afraid of nothing. He would not run away.'

'He had stolen cattle and he also killed one of the sourijs. The sourijs say they are sorry.' Then she added, 'You have nothing to fear.' There seemed to Harib to be little point in arguing the matter. Kara was dead and could not live again. It could hardly have been any fault of the woman's and yet he wondered how she came to be serving the sourijs. 'Come,' she said, 'I will show you the wonderful things that are here.' They went down the ladder, past the sourij at the bottom, and Harib would have stayed to look at the club, but the woman beckoned him on and he followed her across the open space and finally up another short ladder into a new hut. This was not the same as the first one he had been in, but it was again full of strange things. On a platform in the centre were piles upon glittering row of copper plates, necklaces, drinking cups, beads and brightly coloured garment stuffs. There were only two sourijs in the hut and Harib saw that one was the same chief who had met him and his companions earlier.

'Where are the others?' he asked the woman suddenly as he remembered.

'They have gone home,' she said, 'they have gone back to their huts.' Harib looked around him doubtfully, but the sourijs were smiling. One was smoking a pipe, the same as the elder had smoked, and he held it out inviting Harib to take it. Harib puffed and inhaled deeply; he coughed and his eyes watered, but the smoke was not unpleasant and he felt his nerve ends tingling. He sniffed and fingered the tobacco on the table and chewed a little; it seemed rather poor stuff compared with the dagga of the real people. The elder had said so too; there were no dreams to be had from it, nothing to make a man ready to strangle a buffalo with his bare hands or run upon the water or sleep with many women. But perhaps one had to become accustomed to it gradually.

They gave him some of the beads and a few pieces of copper, but he handed them back, telling the woman that he was not willing to trade his charm, and when she explained to him that they were presents he put them solemnly in his pouch. The yellow chunk they gave him to eat was very good and he knew that it was well-prepared sour milk, but the sweet stuff was even more pleasing; as sweet as honey and brown; like wet sand it crunched when he chewed it. He ate only a little of these things, out of politeness, for he did not wish to offend the sourijs and decline their food.

The woman said that he must sit upon the sitting thing and listen, so he sat gingerly on the edge, and then a sourij took an instrument and scraped it with another and a thin noise came from it. It reminded him of the sound of the black, fork-tailed katakroo bird when it swooped to catch bees, and he listened patiently until the sound stopped, beaming and nodding to show his approval. The woman had been talking earnestly to the chief and with the sudden silence Harib felt that he should contribute something to help the laboured meeting along. He said to the woman, 'Soon I will return to my country and when I come again I will bring as many of the heavy pebbles as I can find.'

He waited while she translated. After a while she said, 'The sourij chief thanks you and says that to show his gratitude and friendship he is anxious to send some of his best sourijs to go with you and help you on your journey. They would take much food and drink and presents for your people.'

A shaft of afternoon sun poured into the dank interior setting colours alight and silver points dancing. In his imagination he could see again the mountain stream, amber gleaming between green forest walls; then he thought of Kara and their hunting times at night in the eerie silence of the great forest and then he tried to imagine the giants in the forest and by the streams and the picture would not come. In the wooden house there was suddenly a tense silence. The sourij chief sat looking up at the roof as though an answer would come from there and the woman gazed at the floor. Instinctively he knew that a great deal depended upon his reply. Of one thing he was certain—they would never find the place without him and now that Kara was dead he alone could lead them there. At the same time another thought struck him—if they wanted these pebbles so badly, which seemed to be the case, they would be loath to let him go for fear that he would not come back. He said to the woman, 'Tell the chief that I am grateful to him for his offer but it is very far to go and there are many dangers. One must also go through the country of the Hesaquas and there is warfare between these people and my own. It is better that I go alone. It would not be safe with more than one.' The chief sourij began to rub the black hair below his nose and to drum his fingers on the wood before him.

A cup had been poured and the woman offered it to

23

Harib. 'This is the best drink,' she said. 'Only the greatest in the land of the sourijs drink such fine stuff.' Harib sniffed and tasted; it was much sweeter than the last and very pleasant to taste, less strong. He sipped cautiously, watching the chief with quick brown eyes. Presently the woman said, 'The sourij chief asks if there is anything you would like to see; you have only to say.' She paused. Harib drained the cup and licked his lips. She smiled at him.

'The fire weapons,' he said. 'I would like to see the weapons and to see the smoke and fire they can make.' His request caused a stir and he listened to the quick angry sounding talk of the sourij chief and saw some of the sourijs move outside and for a moment he was afraid that he had angered the giants. But the woman smiled at him again and beckoned him to follow as she led the way out into the afternoon sun, while all the sourijs gathered behind, talking and waving their hands. They descended the wooden ladder and Harib could see one of the sourijs with bright clothes holding a fire club and walking towards the wall of the great house. Behind him the sourij chief was still talking to those others in black clothes; black as crows, Harib thought, like the black crows with white collars around their necks. He watched intently, but he was too far away to see what the giant was doing with the club. He was making strange motions with his hands over the weapon and presently he took a thin stick and pushed it down inside the weapon and then he touched the end with his hand and once more pushed the stick inside. Now he put the stick into the ground and placed the weapon upon it. Then he made a swift movement with one hand and Harib heard a scraping sound and saw a wisp of smoke. Somehow fire

24

had appeared and the sourij was putting it into the club. He craned forward. One of the sourijs in black spoke and the giant with the weapon put his head down beside it and his hands and arms upon it like a maiden upon a praying rock, and Harib could only be sure that somehow the great fire of the stormy sky was being called down by magic to the command of these strange beings. If these giants could call upon the great S'Humma for the loan of his storm fire then indeed they were not men, not giants even, but gods themselves.

'Watch now,' the woman beside him said. Harib licked his lips and nodded, but his eyes had not once left the giant and the weapon with its faint wisp of blue smoke. He was aware of a silence, then the quick, angry voice sounded again, and as he watched there came from the end of the club a spurt of smoke faster than his eye could believe and with it a sound so loud that he fell back and crouched down with an arm flung over his head; but the sound died slowly and when the last reverberating echoes had gone his ears could no longer serve him true in remembering how loud and sharp the sound had been. Like a heavy stone striking another but far, far louder; like the thunder of the sky when the fire of S'Humma sprang and flashed and shook among the clouds. The weapon was there in the same place with the giant behind it, but a cloud of smoke hung silent and ominous over it and Harib rose very slowly to his feet. He stood close to the woman and looked at her for the first time in many minutes. He said 'Hou' with great emphasis and then they both laughed. The black-clad figures were walking towards the wall, and the woman followed, telling Harib to look. 'See,' she said, pointing to a thick piece of wood leaning against the sunbaked plaster. 'See the hole? That is where the heavy stone from the weapon was flung. See, it went right through. It could go through a lion also or a man.' One of the black-clad figures held out his hand and in it Harib saw a small grey ball, round as a berry. Gingerly he took it and was surprised by its weight. 'That is the same as the one that came out of the weapon with the smoke and the fire,' the woman said. Harib weighed the ball in his hand. Its weight reminded him of the yellow stone at the end of his necklace and it dawned upon him that the giants must want the yellow stones for their weapons. But somehow the connection seemed far fetched; the yellow stones were heavy but they were not round.

The black-clad figures walked slowly ahead, deep in conversation, and Harib ambled along with the girl. The sun, he noticed, was already far down on the horizon and he could hear the sound of cattle lowing somewhere beyond the wall. Soon it would be dark and he was undecided about his future movements, but he was no longer afraid. At least the girl was of his own kind and he could sense in her a sort of sympathy. The thought of spending a night here in this vast house of magic filled him only with curiosity and excitement, so he walked with the slow swaggering gait of the black-clad giants, feeling quite tall and even a little proud. If only his own people could see him now.

The chief sourij was still talking earnestly to another when they re-entered the small house and when the girl joined them Harib was left to stare about him in a conscious effort to understand something of the complicated world around him. His attention was first drawn to a tall shiny box of sharp angles which stood in a dark corner. Even above the hum and grumble of the voices he could hear a ticking rhythm, the heartbeat of a live thing; the sound became louder as he drew nearer and then he saw the moving tail swinging slowly back and forth, a live thing in a shiny box; his eyes opened wide and he backed away. Turning, he faced a second shiny thing as round as the moon and shiny as the sea with the moon upon it and as he passed slowly he found to his surprise that it was in fact a hole in the side of the house and that he was looking into another house beyond. Then he saw black-clad figures and they were familiar and then a girl in a coloured garment and finally, with the sheer terror of a nightmare, the face of a real person ducked out and peered at him with wide, startled eyes. For a second he stared in fascinated horror at the face with its slowly opening mouth, then he bounded back with a cry of alarm. The two sourijs and the girl were looking at him in silence and he turned to them with some relief. At least they were the devils he knew. The girl suddenly began to giggle and crossing to him she took his arm and led him to the hole. He went reluctantly and even more gingerly he allowed her to take his hand and to touch it against a cold hard surface. He closed his eyes. He opened one cautiously. Now he could see the girl in the shiny thing and yet she was still beside him. The man standing next to her was himself. Like the reflection in a clear mountain stream he saw himself but many times clearer and brighter. Wonder upon wonder. How beautiful he was. He smiled and then he laughed and the girl laughed and he saw suddenly how bright her teeth were, almost as white as his own. The black-clad sourijs were laughing too and his fear evaporated like water in a fire.

With a cup of the strong honey drink once more in

his hand Harib was suddenly happy to talk to the girl and the two sourijs. Much of the earlier strain had gone with their laughter and while the chief had again asked to see the necklace, now he seemed genuinely interested in hearing more of Harib's country and his people. He told them of the Hesaqua war and of the many cattle which the Hesaqua had and how his own people were hunters, fishermen and gatherers of food by the sea. He told them of the great herds of buffalo and elephants and eland, of the black-maned lions who preyed upon the herds, but always when he and the girl forgot the sourijs and talked of the small things that were as bright as stars to the real people, so that the girl laughed as he mimed with his hands and his body, the chief would cough and move and then the talk would be of the yellow pebbles and where they lay and how many days' journey he had travelled and where was the sun as he faced the sea and how high were the mountains.

During the meal that followed, with little fires burning on the wooden platform and with such a dancing of colours that Harib was reminded of lourie feathers and oyster shell and the stones that one could look through, he had another shock. Two men or devils, he knew not which, came bearing bowls of food and they had skins that were as black as the charcoal of an old fire, as black and shiny as the black snakes of the grasslands, blacker than the forest water. They were big too, these strangers, and the muscles of their almost naked bodies seemed filled with strength. Harib stared in amazement. For a moment he had thought that they were real people or sourijs who had smeared themselves with fat and powdered charcoal. But the black skins were natural and so were their strangely different faces with the thick lips;

28

only their hair was familiar, short with tight little buttons of black fuzz like the hair of the real people. A chord in his memory stirred, for he had once heard of such men who lived far away beyond the forests of the north and it was said that they ate the flesh of their own kind. How powerful then were these sourij giants who could make slaves of such man-eaters?

As the evening progressed, it became hotter and stuffier and Harib found that he could no longer sit still in comfort, for the platform seemed to revolve and the little fires were everywhere, like fireflies in a forest. He had talked a great deal, he knew, and he had danced and fallen down, and now a lassitude was descending upon him. He was dimly aware of movement and strong arms supporting him and the cold blackness of the night, like icy water, and then suddenly he was waking in the vaguely familiar wooden-walled room with the single high window and its shaft of daylight. For many minutes he lay staring up at the grey ceiling, telling himself that in a moment he would awake to the sound of the sea or the rustle of a forest. But no sound came. No bird, no boom of the ocean, no grass or fire scent, only the mustiness of the wooden prison and the sickly smell of rotting cabbage and the faint scrabbling of a rat's claws as it scurried away from the movement of his hand. And yet it must be a dream. In a kaleidoscopic jumble he saw again the looming sourijs, the smoking weapon, the long spears for stabbing, the colours, the live thing in a box, the black slaves, the strange flavours of new food and drink, the vastness of the great house. It was too much. His head ached and he lay back and closed his eyes. It occurred to him that he might be dead and all at once he was homesick. He sat up and actually touched himself to

29

make certain that he was physically intact and then, with a renewal of energy and cheerfulness that made him forget his headache, he resolved to go home. Perhaps he would come back one day with some of the yellow pebbles, but certainly not soon. He had enough stories to tell for a lifetime and life had suddenly become very precious. The sourij giants had passed so far beyond the limit of his understanding that they might as well have come from the stars and an instinct was telling him that the real people must either change like the girl had done or go far away beyond the giants' ken; the alternatives would be madness and a death like Kara's or decay and a kind of slavery, for nothing could withstand the magic of beings who could harness the fire and the thunder of the sky.

He waited for the girl and time passed slowly. He ate a piece of brown loaf and drank water from an earthenware pot. In one corner he found an empty receptacle which seemed to be made of wood and after some deliberation he urinated into it, then he slept again. He was awakened by the sounds of footsteps outside and scrambled to his feet. Sunlight flooded his darkness as the girl came in with a halo of colour. She brought a dish of cooked meat and an earthenware pitcher of milk. She placed these on the platform and then looked at him, her head on one side, her hands on her hips.

'You drank too much wine again,' she said, but her eyes twinkled and Harib merely shook his head as if to rid himself of the memory. 'I have brought you food, for you are surely hungry. It is good meat.' She helped herself to a piece and munched contentedly. Harib needed little urging and from the size of the platter he could see that the girl had brought more than enough for both of them. They ate in silence for a while, quite unselfconsciously.

After a time Harib said, 'Soon I must go back to my own country.'

The girl nodded slowly but said nothing; she reached for another piece of meat. She knew what he meant.

'And you?' he asked.

The girl licked her fingers. 'They call me Tassie,' she said, 'but I am "bright shell from the deep water". I am of the third family of the second tribe of "man too big for hole" who was the son of "many feathers" who was the son of "running too fast for lion" who was the chief of the Chariguriquas. My family are Goringhaikonas and we live here close to the big house. We do not hunt or fish now. We help the sourijs. I have no home place.' She paused. Then she said wistfully, 'You have a good place to live in.' Some of the supper-time conversation was beginning to come back to him and he remembered now that he had talked a great deal about his beloved birthplace and its beauty. The girl saw him wrinkling his brow in an effort to remember and she laughed. 'You do not remember,' she said, 'but you told me many things.' Then more seriously she added, 'And the sourij chief, you told him that you would lead his men to the yellow pebbles. Even now they are preparing.'

Harib chewed reflectively. He did remember and it had not been a drink-inspired decision. His overriding consideration was to get away from the so far tender but firm clutch of the giants, and he knew that the only way to bring this about was to co-operate initially. Once away from the great house, he would be the eyes of the expedition and he had yet to decide for whom his eyes would work. He wiped his mouth with the back of his hand. He was surprised to hear that preparations were already under way. The unnatural interest of the giants in the yellow pebbles continued to amaze him, but such alacrity pointed to something rather more serious than mere interest and he became aware of new misgivings. He said to the girl only, 'It is good that they are preparing, for I cannot stay here longer.' Then he added, 'I am grateful to you, Tassie, perhaps one day I will come back.'

The girl shrugged her shoulders. She kept her eyes downcast and scratched with her nail on the table; then she looked up and Harib saw for the first time a seriousness and a wistfulness that he would not have suspected. 'I do not think you will come back,' she said. 'The sourijs can give many things, but they will benefit you little. Already they kill cattle for the ships faster than they can breed. When all the cattle have been bought then our people must either live like the bush people on the game they can catch or work for the sourijs in return for food. Already some of the chiefs have become like children with wild honey, in their liking for tobacco and arrack and bread.'

Harib rubbed his chin thoughtfully. The girl was very young and it seemed strange that he was seeing her only now for the first time. 'You speak wisely for one so young,' Harib said, studying her face and finding it gave him pleasure to look at her. 'The sourijs have taught you well.'

'I have learned much from them,' she said, 'and they have been good to me. It is true that they do not wish to harm the real people. But there are bad ones amongst them. One will be with you on your journey. He is smaller than the others and speaks with a thin voice, his

32

hair is black and he has much hair on his face. You must be careful of him.'

Harib nodded. 'Again I thank you.' Then he said thoughtfully, 'It is a long way and there are dangers enough, how could it profit them to harm me?'

'I cannot say, but I feel it. Many times before I have heard talk of this yellow heavy stuff, and it seems that the sourijs value it even more than cattle.' A silence fell between them as Harib's mind moved like a fast bird over the mountain ranges and the rivers. Then he said musingly, 'I must find my weapons.'

'I will send for them,' Tassie said quickly. 'I know where they are.'

In the brilliant sunshine outside the fort Harib and the girl stood together as though they were no part of the bustle around them. The sourijs seemed so big and noisy, so brash and angry, they dominated everything. A nucleus of slender brown bodies was beginning to grow with the excitement of voices and protesting oxen. The hooves of the oxen slithered and scuffled as the pack beasts wheeled and shied at their loads and leather lashings. Harib looked around him for the elder and his brother and the rest of his companions, but they were nowhere to be seen. The woman Tara was also missing. Then a young boy pushed through the crowd and touched Harib's elbow and he was overjoyed to find that the boy had brought his weapons. All his stone-tipped arrows were there safe in their hide quiver; and his long spear with the bone head and the bow so polished from his hand.

Harib leaned on his spear and chatted to the girl while the interminable preparation continued. After a while they went away and sat together. Tassie pointed, 'That is the one I spoke of.' She indicated a figure by the oxen.

'I see him,' Harib said, nodding. 'It is good that you have told me.'

As they watched, the sourij chief began to make his way towards the nucleus of the rapidly gathering crowd and a lane parted for him and the two who followed. Harib looked in bemused wonder at the colourful blending of sourijs, real people and black slaves, with here and there the silver water flash of a weapon and the darting of a child, and over all the low hum of different tongues. For a while he had thought that the entire crowd was to come on the journey and he had shaken his head and said to the girl that the expedition might just as well not begin, for it would never reach its destination, but she had told him that there would be six sourijs only and one other real person who could speak some of the sourij language. They would travel with two oxen and this time Harib's doubts were not so easily dispelled. He was almost certain that the oxen would never reach even the fringes of the Outanqua country. If they were lucky enough to survive the lions and the mountains and the rivers the Hesaquas would assuredly not let such heavily laden prizes slip through their hands.

When the sun was high up over the sea, lighting the towering wall of the mountain with the reds and greys of ancient rock and the purple and mauve of gorge or cleft and washing its base with a deep green of forest, the oxen began to move. The girl looked at Harib with luminous eyes. 'Go safely, Harib Outanqua, I know you.'

Harib smiled and touched her hand. He said, 'I will find you, Kahaia Goringhaikona.'

Slowly, the running children and their excited dogs

fell away behind and for a long time Harib could see the girl standing alone by the wooden palings of the cattle enclosure, then the great house was obscured by a line of sand-dunes and the wild land as far as he could see lay lonely and unsullied around him.

3

At the end of the second day the expedition had begun
to settle into a vague pattern. The oxen, nervous and
wild at first and bucking under their shifting loads, had
been coaxed and beaten into submission; they plodded
doggedly now, with wide eyes and low swinging heads,
and Harib was more than ever certain that the beasts
would never survive the journey. At his instigation a
good weight of copper plate had been unpacked and
cached for the return journey, but many miles lay
ahead.

It had rained steadily and the mood of the expedition had changed swiftly from one of expectation buoyed with hope and excitement to a silent shuffle of discomfort and dejection. Ahead of them loomed the first mountain wall, ending the farthest beaten track from the great house and beginning a chapter of unexplored wilderness for the sourijs. As darkness approached, they made camp by a bushy knoll on the banks of a stream and off-loaded the oxen. They made a rough circle of thorn bushes and rope as a crude 'skerm' against lions and leopards and lit their fires. As night fell, the rain stopped and a full flush of stars lit the mountains with ghostly light. The sourijs rattled their cooking implements and smoked their pipes. There was a smell of food and tobacco smoke and a whiff of rum; there were rumbling voices and there was laughter. Harib, sitting under a dark-leaved branch with Hola the interpreter, poked their fire until its lambence enveloped them like a red cloak. They talked of many things and watched the sourijs, more giant-like with the shadows of their fire, more loud in the night, more kind in the night, almost human. Each night two of them would stand guard with the little strings of their weapons smoking and glowing in readiness. But Harib and Hola were content to be by themselves and to sleep deeply; like cats under their sheepskins, like swift brown antelope under the bushes waiting for the sun.

There was no moon and it was very still. The rum Harib had drunk made him drowsy and light-headed but he listened almost unconsciously to every sound that reached his ears and there were many. He heard them all and registered them: the coughing of quagga and the sudden snort of a hartebeest; then the long howling ululation of a hyena. Once he heard the sharp whistle of a startled rhebuck and then later the soft sighing grunt of a leopard.

In the first stages of the journey the game herds had been small and isolated, with here and there a rhinoceros and now and then a party of eland or hartebeest, but the herds had been wary and man-shy. Even the ostriches and oryx had blended with the land and disappeared as the cavalcade moved by. Not a single shot had been fired so far and Harib was impatient to see the fire weapons in action. But during the afternoon, as they moved into the valleys below the mountains, the plains had begun to blaze with life and where such herds roamed the lions would be also. He was listening, he knew, for a lion, but the sound did not come; only the day came, a brilliant sunrise of a day, the day for a mountain, and he arose refreshed and happy. Beyond the mountain, far, far away, was his own land and he was coming home. As far as the sourijs were concerned he was content to let destiny take the lead.

As he went down to the river a herd of hartebeest whirled away from the water, galloped, jumped, rattled stones and was gone. Water seeped like blood into spoor in the wet sand; in the wet sand also was the fresh spoor of a lion and he went cautiously from instinct, pausing to listen to the waking sounds of the camp. A covey of bush francolin clucked and tinkled away into silence through the reeds, telling him that the lion had gone, for the presence of the herd was no guarantee of safety, and a thwarted lion would very quickly kill a man. He bent over the water to drink and something very gentle and yet significant seemed to be wrong; then he felt with his hand and looked down and found that the little heavy

39

pendulum around his neck was missing; it was gone. He sat down on the sand and looked over each shoulder in turn. He felt with his hand again and looked about him on the sand. He searched in his leather pouch and even in the shred of leather about his loins in case it had fallen there. He peered down into the water of the stream, but he knew that he had lost his charm, his golden eland, and, as though a shadow had crossed the sun, a sudden unravelling of superstition shadowed his mind and his eyes.

He searched the camp and the place where he had slept and it was inconceivable that anyone would have stolen such a thing; in the realms of the real people a man's personal charm could be a deadly thing in the hands of another. And yet he was certain that he had not lost it on the way. Hola showed great concern at the news of the missing necklace. Harib told him as they picked their way up a boulder-strewn gorge ahead of the oxen and the cloud of melancholy superstition he wore afterwards was genuine enough; no real person in his right mind would take the talisman of another unless it was a gift. If one of the sourijs had it, then it could be dangerous for them all, for they were a knit and interdependent unit, a single thing in terms of the land. They discussed the possibility at length.

By now all the giants had become identities. There was Black, the small dark high-voiced one, the one Harib had been warned about. There was Eland Bull, the leader, a red-faced giant with hair the colour of butter flowers. There was Hyena, who had protruding teeth and a wide mouth and a big shaggy head, who spoke loudly and laughed a great deal; he also ate noisily and seemed to enjoy his food more than the others. There was Ashgrey, who said little and was always behind; he had grey hair and was older. The fifth was Polecat because he smelled more than the others, and the sixth was Frog, short and square with bandy legs.

Eland Bull was the one they saw most. He spoke with a slow, low voice and the others listened to him. His eyes were a pale blue-green and when he smiled they lit with a glint like sea water over coral in the sun. He carried a long knife in his belt as well as a short fire weapon and wore garments that blended with the land; each night he would sit a little apart from the others for a while and spread a flat white square upon a box across his knees and with a goose quill between his fingers he would paint upon the white surface; but there were never pictures, only lines of marks like the ones the women of the real people made around their clay pots. Eland Bull never raised his voice and when he beckoned to Harib or spoke to Hola it was with the same gentleness he used with the others. Black, on the other hand, was quick and impatient and loud as an angry crow. He seemed to regard the expedition as his own personal venture and clamoured at delays and mishaps. Sometimes Eland Bull would speak only a little, softly, and Black would cease his restless chatter and mutter with a sickly smile. Once Harib watched him grimace behind Eland's back, but only Polecat allowed his eye to be caught and to share the smirk.

Harib toiled ahead up the ever steepening slope of the mountain. He had explained to Hola and watched the interpretation to Eland that the way they were travelling was new to him, but a logical connection with his old route not too many miles away. The detour was necessary because of the oxen, for he had come close to the sea on his journey to the great house and no ox could climb where he had climbed. They were crossing a shallow ravine which higher up, Harib could see, narrowed to a steep cleft, for he was thinking like an ox; he was watching from above and across the gully when the black mane of the lion seemed to light all the dead bushes and the dead rock with dangerous life, like a beautiful woman suddenly amongst men or a shark turning grey light in sheltered water or an arrow shaft aching in a shoulder under unbelieving eyes. It was too quick for Harib to shout more than once, the spring of the long yellow body, so brilliant in the sunlight among the red bushes and the flowers. He could only hear his voice trailing away like an echo of the lion's power and see white frozen faces looking up and hear the dull thud of flesh as the lion struck the leading ox and watch the ox and the lion tumble together amidst a clatter of baggage over a ledge and away below. All the suddenness of fear in Harib's heart seemed to flash to his legs and his brain and in a wild leap, spear in hand, he followed the lion and the ox over the bushy edge, seeing Eland drawing his short fire weapon as he passed but thinking only of the muscles of his body and the sharp extension of his arm as a means of killing, and he yelled into the lion's yellow eyes, as they glowed at him for a second; for the ox was his, his feet and eyes were the eyes and feet of the oxen, he had walked and seen for them. What slothful lion could take them for himself, and he yelled and hurled his spear, but the lion turned and in another bound was gone. Harib stood still over the fallen ox. Slowly he became aware of a man's breathing beside him and then the dark rod of Eland's fire weapon and Eland's brick-red hand came into the field of his vision. They glanced at each other, like a flash of fire the eyes, and then they looked together at the feet under the spine of the motionless ox.

It was Ashgrey and he was alive when they rolled the dead ox from his chest, but he breathed with pain and there was blood on his lips. They carried him carefully into a corner of level ground and sat beside him and then they foraged for the things that the red ox had carried: flasks and pouches, bags and bales, and night fell eventually and their fire burnt like an exotic ruby upon the slope of the mountain.

In the morning Ashgrey died, the oldest and the most harmless. Perhaps that was the way, Harib thought, the way the evil of the charm would work. Eland Bull looked worn and tired and Harib knew that he had not slept. What a thing it would have been to see the short fire weapon flaming and roaring against the lion. What a thunder the two would have made. But the fire weapon slept while Eland drew his pictures and even Black and Hyena were silent. They buried Ashgrey under a cairn of rocks and then divided up amongst them as much as they could carry of powder and lead and provisions. But Harib, busy skinning the ox, did not know why they should concern themselves with any of the things that the ox had carried, for the ox was food for days and were not all the possessions concerned eventually with food? At a new camping site a short way up the slope of the mountain from where Ashgrey was buried they stopped because Hyena was ill and could go no further, but Harib and Hola were not displeased, for there was meat to be eaten until they could eat no more and Hyena seemed to recover quickly, for he too ate his share.

The mountain trapped them for three days amongst

its grey rock walls and wire-hard scrub and all the while, as they toiled and cursed beside the straining ox, they were haunted by the memory of the lion and Ashgrey alone and rain cold in his stone grave. On the afternoon of the fourth day, with a salty wind blowing welcomingly across the last spur of the mountain top, they looked out over undulating plains rolling blue and grey into the distance, while the sea filled all the southern horizon and a barrier chain of mountains in the north, marched peak upon peak to where eyesight and the sea and the plains ended. Harib leaned on his spear and waited for the ox and the exhausted men to rest. He was becoming impatient with the endless delays and the snail's pace of the journey; alone he would by now have been far beyond where the eye's reach ended, across the two rivers and perhaps on the fringes of Hesaqua country. But the giants were themselves in a way like lumbering animals under all the impediments they carried and he was experiencing a growing sense of responsibility for them. He was no longer afraid; indeed, he felt a kindness for them and a genuine liking, especially for Eland and Polecat and even Hyena. Black he could not enjoy and Frog was difficult to like. But he was a worried shepherd, for there were dangers ahead and the giants seemed so helpless and wretched here under the open sky. If the Hesaquas made running or hiding necessary, then he could see no escape; but they had far to go yet and the fire weapons were powerful and marvellous.

Since the loss of the charm, Harib had been deeply suspicious of Black. He had watched him and followed him with his eyes often and sometimes he had sensed the other's discomfort, but things had gone smoothly since the death of Ashgrey, and Harib and Hola were both agreed that perhaps the full price had already been paid. Eland had quickly felt the uneasiness of the two real people, but he could do nothing; he could accuse nobody, nor could he subscribe to Hola's premonition of disaster. The incident had been deliberately dismissed and Harib could only wonder and frown as they sat in the evenings around their ever lonelier fires, when the coals smouldered flameless, and talking gave way to lonely thought.

Now, with the mountain behind them, it was as though the chapter of the charm with the death of Ashgrey had ended and they went down to a camp beside a stream amongst a green thicket with more speed and enthusiasm than Harib had thought possible. The giants were happy under the black trees by the tinkling water and Harib and Hola edged closer to their fire, closer to the circle of laughter, radiant and compelling as a woman. Harib listened to their talk and though he could understand nothing, the mime of their faces was entertainment enough. They had eaten the last of the ox and they had drunk a ration of arrack. Eland, like a chief, said little, but he smiled and listened and laughed softly sometimes and then his voice would rumble in a silence that seemed to have been waiting for him and then the others in turn would talk and move their faces and hands with the lore of story-telling which Harib knew so well. The giants possessed a magnetic quality and in being drawn to them he could only believe that because they were gods he was drawn. But could gods die or be as clumsy and as inept as these when there was no more laughter?

The night was warm and there was little sound except for the frogs and crickets that filled all their ears with a strangely lulling music under the canopy of smoke and

45

glow that marked the circle of their camp. Beginning to sleep, Harib listened to a distant rumbling so far away that it could have been either a quagga or a lion or a hippopotamus or even a buffalo; then a jackal yapped and howled close by. The jackal in the manner of a jackal and by his long low sob of a howl told Harib that all was well and, like a sentry going off duty, he was quickly asleep.

The plains, which from the top of the mountain had looked so flat and soft to the giants, silenced them soon, as Harib knew they would. The valleys, shallow as they may have seemed from the mountain top, were steep-sided and stony and the long gradients perpetual switch-backs, energy-sapping under a glaring sun. In these foothills of the mountain range they came upon immense herds of game. Hartebeest and zebra, quagga and buffalo, bontebok and eland whirled and cantered in confusion as firelocks flashed and roared in the virgin wastes. Harib yelled in excitement, dancing with delight, his hands over his ears and his own weapons forgotten. There was no shortage of food.

Hyena, following a wounded hartebeest that limped away tossing its head one afternoon, cried out suddenly in fear and dropped his weapon. Harib, skinning a big buck with Eland Bull, looked up and saw him running and thinking of lions he reached for his spear and stood while Eland drew the short fire weapon from his belt. Eland Bull called across the little valley, but the running giant, stumbling blindly now, gave no answer and the veld gave no hint of danger. He panted up to them, his eyes wide with terror, and stood swaying with exhaustion and holding his wrist. Harib could only listen to the words he spoke and see the expression on Eland's face, but a glance was enough. The white inner flesh on Hyena's arm showed bulging blue veins from the pressure above where he gripped with a great red hand, but there was a leak of blood like a thorn wound, smeared, and another where a welling drop formed, and Harib knew the marks of a snake. Quickly they tied a thong around the stricken giant's arm, twisting it tight at the pulse above the elbow with a stick, and as Eland sharpened the point of his knife, Harib held out to him a little razor-sharp sliver of crystal from his pouch, and when Eland nodded quickly he slashed into the white skin down the arm towards the hand and then again over the fang punctures. They were wide apart, the innocent-looking little holes, it meant a big snake; Harib was thinking as Hola and Frog came running to them, a yellow cobra or a puff-adder, and if one of the fangs had pierced the blue vein, then the giant carried death within him. They knelt beside him in the stony patch and spoke worriedly; only Harib was silent, watching the blood glistening wetly and drying at the edges; watching the pulsing vein and watching powerless as the hand began to swell. They loosened the thong a little after a while, for it was biting deep into the puffed flesh and when the giant tried to sit up they could see that his eyes were losing their power; he blinked at them, trying to focus, and his head lolled as though he was drunk and the powerful hands were limp as a child's. After a while his eyes closed and the laboured breathing became slower, and as though all the muscles in the great body were failing, his chest grew still at last and they knew that he was dead.

Harib had seen men die before but never from the bite of a snake. He tried to rationalise his emotions in terms of this and succeeded in some way but not completely, for Hyena's death seemed to bring a shiver of cold wind and a masking of the sun and a draining of colour from the living bushes. Before it was dark the rain had started and they went away from the grave and the pile of stones, knowing that it was too shallow for beasts of prey but that they were cold and wet and dispirited and could do no more. They cowered from the rain and the wind under an overhanging ledge of shingle, watching the bushes hiss and bend and the raindrops flurrying. The ox moved and moaned at its tether and Eland sat with his chin on his arms and his arms wrapped around his knees while the smoke of the fire swirled into his face, but he only closed his eyes until the cloud had turned to attack another, and remained motionless.

It rained throughout the night and all the next day and they plodded slowly through dongas beginning to run with water; the plains seemed deserted, but once they were forced to detour around a glowering rhinoceros under a low tree; the ox bellowed and the glistening beast with its strident horn sniffed and listened, pawing the wet earth and peering myopically into the torrent as they passed. It rained through the night as they cringed under the cover of trees deep down in a valley that smelled of damp earth and with a stream cascading ever louder. There was no other sound but the rushing and beating of water. Harib and Hola, side by side under their sheepskins, spoke little and the giants were silent. But at midnight the rain ceased suddenly, and very slowly, above the roaring of water, the grumbling, swaggering grunting of a lion invaded their misery. Those who had been asleep awoke quickly as another lion took up the chorus and then another, until the night reverberated with bellow upon grunting, whooping bellow. Harib felt an eerie terror that was new to him. Carefully he had led the expedition diagonally across the foothills of the mountains away from the sea, away from the territory of the Hesaquas, and now, as the mountains slanted back with the curve of the coast, they were entering the region of dry aloe thickets, with here and there a spur of forest from the wet mountains. The rain was something he had not expected and nor were the lions. This was the area of buffalo and leopard, of mountain eagle and the slow-witted grey antelope with the curving horns. It was also an area of deep ravines with water pools waiting to become rivers, hoping for rain. As the lion chorus waxed and waned, the giants struggled with their fire weapons while Harib coaxed a sodden fire into life and Hola and Frog tried to calm the plunging ox. The darkness was confused, but running through Harib's head as he crouched blowing into the living heart of the black heap was the suspicion that somehow the rain had taken away the magic of the weapons as it could quell the flames of a bush fire. He watched as Eland pointed his weapon into the dark sky and saw sparks, but the weapon remained silent. A flicker of lightning crackled across the sky and to Harib, Eland was a towering giant in the blue light of tumbling clouds. He said two words in explosive anger and again sparks flew and again the lions blared with voices of blood, like drums and wind on the sea. Eland fumbled with the other magic things of the weapon; the round shining thing like a gourd with the black powder and the long thin rod and when he held the weapon again it flashed and roared at the sky and the lions as though it were spitting out all the anger and the fear of the camp. Harib fell back in supplication, pleased and yet afraid, and then he saw the ox break loose; in the half-light of their camp it was gone in an instant, but they heard it tearing and crashing through the bush towards the lions and the camp became silent, without movement, slowly as they listened; the giants and the two real people froze into statues as quiet as the lions had become and waiting, while the sounds of the ox became fainter and fainter and at last, because they knew it had to come and because they too wanted its death and the finality of its death like a scapegoat, they seemed to sigh when the last, frantic, single bellow of the beast had died away.

Black was the first to move. His voice rose into shrill hysteria and Harib felt instinctively for his spear as the man leapt across the stream and stood crouched with his arm outstretched pointing at him and yelling. He could understand nothing and yet he knew what the little giant was saying and what ailed him, but he knew also that if he gave rein to the anger which welled up in him, then he and not Black would die. But he rose slowly and slammed his spear into the ground before him so that it stood dark and poignant in its swift menace and its sudden harmlessness. With the veins in his neck bulging, he shouted into Black's face, 'I did not ask you to come; I do not want you to come. Go back home then, you hairy animal.' The looming presence of Eland Bull seemed to drift between them, so slowly did he come, and his silent figure seemed to Harib to be even more dangerous than Black or the lions, but he was glad, and his anger died almost as quickly as it had come. Harib sank down beside the fire and listened to the still angry but more logical flow of Black's words as he appealed and threatened. After a while Eland called to

50

Hola and spoke to him and quickly Hola translated the words to Harib. When he had finished all the giants were silent and the night was quiet after the rain and the lions. Harib spoke quietly. 'Tell Eland Bull,' he said, 'that if I were a stone in a river and if he stepped upon me I would remain steady for him to cross; and if his men stepped upon me I would still remain steady. And if it were in my power to speak to the lions I would tell them to go. And if I could raise Ashgrey and Hyena from the dead then I would go back now in the darkness to do so. And if I know of a safer route and have chosen the more dangerous one then let him kill me now. Tell him I grieve for the sourijs who have died and for the oxen. Tell him also that we travel slowly and heavily and that I warned the sourijs in the big house of the dangers. That is all.'

In the flickering light of the fire Harib watched Eland's face as he spoke and he knew that, in spite of Hola's slow incantation of his words, he had been understood.

4

The little cavalcade crawled like a slow worm across the ridge back of the mountain chain. Below them the slopes fell away into tangled bush forest, with here and there a spur that reached out far into the plains, and beyond the plains lay the glistening expanse of the ocean. Looking ahead from each new peak after the inevitable swooping valley and slow climb up again they could see no end to the chain. Green cauldrons of almost impenetrable bush trapped them often and sometimes they would detour around steep-sided rocky chasms where streams of water cascaded down into some abyss below. The giants were moving at a pace of torturing slowness. The once proud coverings they wore on their bodies and feet were torn and tattered. Their hair was matted and the hair on the faces covered their mouths and chins and necks like a fungus. They walked doggedly, in silence, and Harib knew that they could only trust him and hate him and go where he led. He could sense that even Eland Bull and Hola were beginning to doubt his integrity and he could only repeat that the mountain passage had bypassed the Hesaquas and that while the route was new to him the mountains would take them directly to the stream of yellow pebbles. He tried to explain that his own tribe lived near the sea beyond the Hesaquas and that to reach the pebble streams from the coastal plains would mean a long, difficult journey through thick forest, the haunt of elephant and buffalo. This way, eventually, they would descend upon the place, for the streams rose in the mountains and not far from the range the pebble beds lay hidden in the deep forest. They lived now upon the power of the fire weapons and carried little else besides them; long ago they had shed the last of the trading trinkets and the bread bags and the empty sacks. Behind them they had left a fading trail of buffalo bones and eland horns and the dappled skins of mountain zebras. They had killed baboons and rock rabbits and red-wing partridges and the little mountain antelopes. Harib had brought wild honey and the berries and roots he knew of, but the giants remained listless and dull-eyed in spite of the food. As they penetrated ever deeper into the wild country, so their spirits seemed to decline and it was understandable to Harib in a way. He knew that they knew their vulnerability and that with each step eastwards they committed themselves further from home, deeper into the dangerous maze and more completely into his power. The whole purpose of their journey seemed to become eclipsed by the hypnotic slog of each new day; they walked silently under the glaring light of summer and crouched in silence under what shelter they could find when it rained. Harib pitied them and felt a weight of responsibility that he could not easily define. Had it been within his power to give each of them, even Black, a little of his own untaxed and even increasing stamina and energy, he would have done so. But he could do nothing more than scout the route ahead and lead them at their own pace onwards.

Still far away, but almost visible now through the mist from the sea, the forest was beginning. He showed Eland Bull from the top of a wind-swept peak and the others crowded up straining and suddenly quick in their movements. Eland gazed for a long time, and his eyes, so blue and green that they had astonished Harib when he first saw them, glowed with renewed purpose. That night, under a rocky overhang, there was even some laughter in spite of an icy wind that howled and screamed at them like a black mountain eagle.

Always when Harib awoke in the morning he found the giants awake before him and during the day sometimes when they stopped to rest they would nod and fall asleep. When Harib gnawed hungrily at his meat the giants ate with little appetite. It was a puzzle to him and increased his belief that they were from a world that bore little resemblance to the one of the real people. Perhaps in their world he would be the same, he did not know. With the forest lands of the Outanqua people coming closer, it seemed to dawn upon the giants that their journey could have a purpose after all and even a reward. As the flat coastal plains shrank and contracted into deep valleys of green, cut by many rivers, so the ocean reached closer and the mountain slopes rose ever steeper and the forests covered all the land as far as they could see. Once, in a clearing below them, an island of yellow, they saw a herd of elephants, tiny grey dots with the white sun-glint of tusks, and once a long line of buffalo stretching from one forest patch, down a valley and up into another. The folds of the mountain ranges were flushed yellow and red with flowers and every bush bore its share of blue or yellow or red, so that the very air seemed coloured and scented with honey.

Harib checked their position with great care. From this angle it was difficult to be certain of the stream and once in the great forest they could stumble blindly without direction for days if they were to choose the wrong one. But at last he was sure and they began the slow descent, slipping and clinging to bushes for support, pausing to rest from the new muscle-torturing tension of bracing instead of pushing upwards, and hour by hour the mountain loomed higher above them and the forest rose up to meet them with a sound of water and the smell of dampness and decay. Near the end of the spur, the bush covering of the slope grew more dense until they were fighting their way through a matted lattice-work of stems close together at the base and bushy tips reaching far over their heads. Harib, in the lead, tore his way with agonising slowness towards the running water he could hear somewhere ahead. The deep shadow of the mountain had long ago engulfed them, but it was as though the air was darkening still more with the almost suffocating heaviness of the forest and then suddenly, with only a hint of changing undergrowth, he burst through the last barrier of wet fern and emerged upon the white sandy shore of a river. The giants staggered out of the green tunnel like strange shaggy beasts and for a while they sprawled thankfully on the sand among smooth white boulders. The water was the colour of honey where it flowed over stony rapids and where it touched the deep base of a cliff farther up on their side it was black as charcoal. Opposite them was another small open space of sand fringed with lush undergrowth and beyond that they could see nothing but the looming oppressiveness of the great forest. A profound silence lay upon the river and all that surrounded it; the river itself by its melancholy tinkle lent depth and perspective to the silence, and the bell of a bird that tolled far away to its distant mate was the forest measuring its time in eternity.

The wind that had blown gently all day from the deserts of the north left a pool of unnatural warmth that flowed about them above the river and then settled with the setting sun softly over them. Eland Bull long ago stirred, curious and striding, crossed the river stones and knelt to wash his face. Then he peeled off the garments from his chest as Harib watched and the garments from his legs and lowered himself into the soft, dark water, blowing and laughing; Harib could only marvel at the stark whiteness of his skin against the green black of the forest and the red black of the water and laugh to see the great muscles of Eland's back and the long lissom muscles of his legs contort in a child's game among the little fishes of the water. He and Hola sat clasping their knees and laughing in astonishment as the others followed, even Black, and then Frog, who clowned with his pipe and hat and his nakedness in the water, until the brooding wilderness was awakened to the sound of giant hearts so that it seemed doubly quiet in a kind of shocked amazement. But it was only the beginning of night and then when the giant's fires roared upon the cooling sand and they ate the last of their meat and smoked their pipes, ruddy-faced around the blaze, the night of the forest remembered itself and began the murmuring of all its creatures as if to show that it too was alive. Their fire seemed to draw the life of the forest closer, for the wild boar rustled close by in the bracken as Harib raised his finger in mid sentence, listening. Hola sat cross-legged, his eyes glowing with the intensity of the questioning and Harib's new eloquence. The wild pigs stopped in unison and Harib in his mind's eye could see the tusked leader and his twitching nose and his hunting instinct could hardly bear to hear him speak. But the giants were avid and awake with closeness. Every detail of the yellow pebbles, and how they lay, they sought from him. Tomorrow was too far away for them and Harib knew that if his choice of streams was wrong then it was not tomorrow nor the next day but a new moon ahead and the giants would not endure. But at last they slept and the wild pigs slipped silently away and a leopard came to drink, sniffing the strangeness of the air and wondering why a fire should sleep so quietly among the smell of burnt meat. And when a waft of invisible smoke crept into the hollows of the forest a bushbuck tossed his horns and snorted and backed and crashed away. But always when the silence was deepest the tinkling of the river came back.

It was cold in the morning, for a dew had dropped upon the sleepers like a blanket when the warm wind withdrew. They woke early and only Harib knew what the creatures were who awoke with them. He drew pictures in the sand for Eland and Eland corroborated with his own splendid strokes in the wet sand so that Harib laughed with pleasure and astonishment at his knowledge and his keen lines. Hola came to look too, and he clucked his tongue in approval. There was no end to the versatility of the giants, no end to their misery and no end to their playfulness. More than ever he was determined that they should have their pebbles. He told Eland that hunting would be difficult in the forest and that here on the fringes was the place for the killing of game, so they listened as he spoke after Eland had called to them, roughly, and they followed him over the river and through the wet fern thickets until they came to the fresh paths of buffalo. They seemed to respond to the new challenge of hunting blind, trusting him and eager to succeed. But the day grew hot and no buffalo came and the giants became churlish like children and went back to their camp. In the windless heat of the day the forest seemed to subside into quietness; nothing stirred or sounded but the single bell of the bird and once the harsh cry of a baboon from high up on the cliff above them. The giants sprawled on the sand waiting for the afternoon in a kind of fatalistic lethargy and once more the brief flash of enthusiasm which had fired them died as their hunger and feeling of helplessness increased.

Harib, sitting quietly apart with Hola, knew that food was urgently necessary and it hurt him to watch the muscled giants drooping in weakness even, it seemed, as he watched them. Theirs was the bitter exhaustion of both spirit and body. Pressed to the very fringes of endurance, the little disappointment of the morning had been enough of a blow to fell them like overtired children and now the desolation of this deep grave of green mocked them with its whispering invisibility, its lack of escape, its tantalisingly hidden food. If he left them now Harib knew that they would die, for they grew clumsy in their weakness and slow. They were no match for the forest creatures even with their fire weapons. Responsibility weighed heavy and unaccustomed on Harib. If the first blast of a fire weapon did not kill or wound badly, then many hours must pass before another opportunity would come. To move in search of game after the rumbling echoes of a shot was out of the question, for the forest stalker must become a leopard, silent as the shadows, inconspicuous, and already the giants staggered under the weight of their ponderous weapons. Now they could not afford the damage of a shot at a monkey or, even less, at a bush francolin or a red-winged forest lourie. They could not scatter to forage and shoot and Harib and Hola could not leave them and go off in search of the tiny blue antelope with their bows and arrows when there was the chance of using the power of the fire weapons against buffalo; from only one buffalo they could build a food reserve and from it a further stock of birds and small animals to restore them for the last and final effort of their journey.

The giants showed a strange apathy for the final plunge into the forest, towards the goal which had sustained them so far, and Harib suspected that it was not only physical exhaustion which held them captive; if there should be nothing he asked himself in their eyes and in their way of seeking, then they would be truly lost. Like children or lovers they were delaying the final revelation.

Through the afternoon shadows they went again, over

rotting logs and fungus patches and through almost tangible clouds of aromatic scent from the crushed river foliage, they followed Harib's slight figure in single file along the trail. In the damp earth even the feet of the giants were silent, Harib reflected, as he followed the ever deepening game path, but he could hear their breathing and the rustle of their torn rags and every now and again there would come the alien metallic click of metal on metal. How little they had spoken of late, he thought, and how nebulous they had become as individuals. Since long before the forest they had grunted at one another like animals, as though the very air they breathed was precious and to be used grudgingly. Gone were the long rolling sentences which had fascinated him and long gone the sudden laughter; even anger had seeped away and been discarded like the trinkets they had carried and the cooking things and the coverings which had kept off the rain. As all these disappeared Harib had found himself drawn closer and closer to them in an understanding which surprised him. From gods they had become willingly, out of necessity, dogs trotting at his heels, listening to his voice, watching his face, and he felt for them such sadness and compassion that it was almost love. The path before him yielded a constant and detailed picture like a never-ending story.

Since a bow-shot back, where a new path cut into theirs like a living nerve in the flesh of green fern, the marks of elephants had dominated the delicate underplay of antelope and pigs' hooves. Here a broken branch with freshly chewed bark lay amongst trampled stalks. There was a deep trench in the loamy bank where tusks had gouged for roots; great round circles of feet had pressed down into the earth, and the marks were fresh. Harib could smell the elephants and he began to walk cautiously. Behind him the giants had begun to murmur and when he stepped over a pile of droppings, yellow fresh with chewed fern and warm to the touch, he turned to Eland and put one finger to his lips. All of the instructions it was necessary for him to give he gave almost apologetically and always through Eland. During the last weeks he had been so closely and sympathetically with the ever-sharp intelligence of Eland that he could convey everything but the abstract through a kind of sign and facial language which they had perfected between them. He told him now that the elephants could upset their plans for the buffalo, but that there was no danger, and when Eland touched a finger to the unlighted matchcord of his weapon in a question mark he shook his head.

With the fire weapons, Harib had been obliged to adapt himself to a totally new form of hunting. After the initial superstitions dread had passed and he had realised with a long delayed flash of understanding that the fire weapons killed with a round heavy ball, unlike a stone, but flung to wound at a distance like the arrow from his bow; he had come to feel the logic of them and to adapt to them some of the old arrow-hunting principles, but with a new power and new distances and with new speed. There was still the unexplained magic of the fire box and the transferring of a fire to the thin cord of the weapon that coiled like a snake and glowed slowly with smoke, and the final fiery climax as the glowing worm dived into the weapon with a spurt of smoke and sparks, to send the hills reeling with smoke and fire and sound. But the smoking cords could permeate the living air of the forest with danger for sensitive nostrils, so the weapons lay passive and the fire boxes lay dead. This too was a problem, for to deny the weapons their ready smouldering spark of cord was to lose time and was to invoke sound when the box made its snapping prayer to the flame, and of sound and scent it was difficult to choose the more damaging to the hunter.

With the sun long gone behind the serrated peaks of the mountain, the air of the forest seemed to take on a new heaviness, as though the shadow was air itself, becoming mobile and alive under the throbbing heart of green. The path they walked began to curve down and dig deeper into the flesh of the old soil. The walls of bracken and fern and feathery aromatic shrub rose higher and higher and the slim tinkling, rustling, drumming beat of the forest came closer with the loom of the darkening air. They breathed liquorice and aniseed and honey and the breath of moss and stagnant water and then the sound of water tinkling came back like an old friend as the walls of the path spread to become a meeting place of other paths and the river flowed again before them. The main path entered the river across an expanse of white sand, and emerged to curve quite sharply up the wooded slope of the opposite bank and disappear from sight into the shadow of a rock wall. Harib signalled Eland to wait and waded through the shallows to investigate. His bare feet left wet patches on the powdery floor of the trail as he climbed up slowly between high banks, and the fresh dung of many large animals squelched between his toes. There was no doubt that this was an old and regular drinking place for elephants and buffalo and eland and with the depth of the path, the result of many thousands of hooves over many thousands of years and the protecting cliff, a perfect ambush. He went down and beckoned the giants;

all except Eland lay prostrate on the sand and he watched as they waded slowly across.

A breeze was ruffling the tree tops as they climbed into their positions and the whole forest beyond them groaned and murmured, as though impatient for darkness, but there was no living sound; not even the funeral note of the bird, only the grunting of the giants and the gentle patter of falling leaves and the clicking of fire boxes and the clink of metal. Harib stayed close beside Eland and watched as he adjusted the smouldering cord in the serpentlike beak of the fire weapon's mechanism. The little wisps of smoke curled up and then puffed away as tongues of wind caught them and swirled them into the dark green of the forest. The scent of smoke was not good, but Harib could only hope that game would come and that the weapons would do their work. He had done his part and the rest, the mystery of the guns, was Eland's responsibility; but they must be patient, they must wait, they must not shoot too soon, and they must be quiet. All this he told Eland and then through Hola he told him that he must shoot first, the others must wait, the signal would come from him. They lay close together among the boulders and roots and waited.

Far away, in the darkness at the back of his head, and with his eyes tight shut, Harib became aware of a faint, constant slithering sound. It seemed to rise and fall with the surge of the wind, but his heart did not lie, and as its beating increased steadily, so the sound grew until he was certain. He lifted his head and opened his eyes and, as Eland looked at him, he nodded and beckoned sideways. Eland's eyes widened and his bearded chin tilted upwards sharply in excitement, but he looked at Harib again after a while, puzzled, and raised an eyebrow half

64

smiling. Harib held up a finger as though he could show him the sound, but it was a full minute later that the giants heard the buffalo coming. They listened now to a shuffling, rumbling and grunting that filled every space around them like the coming of a storm and their faces strained upwards, open-mouthed and open-eyed as they stretched to listen and to see. A river of shadow-black bodies, the buffalo poured down the path scarcely the length of a fire weapon away and below the hunters; bossed horns flew into view on tossed heads, black backs rippled with muscles, invisible hooves drummed the dust into clouds and the herd flowed on into the water to splash and snort and well over on to the sand beyond. Very lightly Harib touched Eland's arm and saw him swallow and ease himself up on his elbows. The long barrel of the weapon between the stones slid slowly forward, the powerful hands with the covering of yellow hair grasped and tightened. Eland's head hung forward motionless for a long time, as though sinking into death among the matted tresses of hair, and then the cord fell; with it the forest flashed and roared with sound; again a blast crashed, smoke billowed amongst the dust, a new smell; the giants were scrambling to their feet. The river seemed to have become a thing of spray and rainbows, a waterfall of sound, the earth shook as the herd bellowed its wild stampede away from the blood scent of the air. And suddenly the last flying rump was swallowed away into the forest while the sound of the herd's passage faded more slowly and the hunters' voices captured the silence for themselves.

Harib, first over the lip of the path, gave a whoop of joy and plunged his spear into the throat of a bull strugling to rise. Another moaned and floundered into the water while the giants staggered after it, all except Eland, carefully loading his fire weapon with the magic from the flask and standing possessively close to the dead buffalo, close to Harib. They grinned at one another. At the water's edge Eland waited while Black fired his short weapon at the dying animal and Harib saw for the first time the power of fire spurt in the water. Then Eland levelled the long glinting barrel and when the flash had gone away with the sound, and the smoke was drifting upwards, the head of the buffalo slid slowly down into the stillness of the water, bringing back the snicker and chuckle of bubbles over stones and the sighing of the trees.

The giants had not yet gathered to smile and laugh at one another when the elephant towered over them, shattering the crystallising forest with its peal upon peal of trumpeting. Harib saw the raised cobra of a trunk and the spread ears; the sand splashed as it whirled like a dancer, grey-blue as slate, its long, straight yellow tusks thrust out in majesty. He saw the swift, crouching Hola darting across the sand like a forest pixie beneath the massive body and then there was the terrible, purposeful, furtive movement of the great forelegs and the whiplash of the trunk. Sound began and ended. The elephant sent plumes of water cascading into the trees; he was crossing the river; the giants turned and ran and the elephant squashed them like beetles. The dead buffalo swirled and crashed into a bank to flop back and roll. He saw a screaming figure high up over the elephant's trunk briefly, but now he was clawing up the cliff in terror and dimly aware that Eland was near him. As high as he could go, where instinct told him that he was safe, he turned in fascination to watch the real giant's anger. The little eyes sought him out against the cliff and sound reached up to suck him down; again and again the sound came until it could hold no more terror and at last the grey violence wandered away into the forest, shedding its anger on the yielding branches, to the far places where all sound ended. Only then did they dare to come down into the sickening circle; and then, too, Black emerged, crouching and wild-eyed from the trees. The others were dead.

During the night, rain began to fall and the three huddled together on a ledge high up against the cliff. The smoke of their fire swirled in eddying gusts of wind and they ate buffalo tongues ravenously, like animals, while the river chuckled and the forest moved and the blood of their companions below them grew hard and cold as river stones. Rain pounded at the billowing edges of their smoke cloud in a white wall that sparkled against the black void beyond, but they kept dry under the overhanging cliff while the forest roared with sound.

Black, stark in the light of the fire, whimpered and moaned incessantly, and when Eland turned upon him suddenly in anger he looked up as though he had been called kindly by his name and his eyes were wild as fire in the red glow. But slowly the whimpering began again as his head subsided, a falsetto keening, weird and terrifying. And Eland, with his head upon his knees, stared out into the darkness, uncaring at last.

But for the glinting of light on the burnished surfaces of the fire weapons the three were the last or the first in the primordal wilderness of age-old forest. Time ended and time began; they sheltered from the rain in a cave, having killed and eaten their game and having survived. All else shed away and all desires past, they fell asleep like children, curled together for warmth and comfort, and as Harib closed his eyes he remembered the tear-streak going slowly down Eland's cheek like a trickle of gold. He remembered and felt his heart hurt him with pity for such great things lost and reduced to nothing. He wished now that he could speak to Eland. Now at last he knew that these giants were men like himself and that he loved them.

5

After the rain the forest lay immaculate and still. The silence was broken only by the excited chuckling of the river and a whispering patter of drops on dead leaves. Then as the morning sunlight began to probe into its dripping heart with fingers of fire, the birds awoke one by one and the ocean of silence became a sunny, undulating sea of life, quivering and vibrant, with peal upon peal and bell upon bell, with the mellow golding of cuckoo and the raucous chatter of bright louries, but always it seemed, far, far away, as though the place where the

69

men stood was void of life, a vaulted cathedral that encompassed them wherever they moved.

It took time for their fire to burn and there was no flame, only a column of blue going up to ignite itself in the sunlight high among the canopy of leaves, but they charred and toasted their meat and ate in silence. Harib, crouching by the smouldering fire, watched the two giants, but they seemed scarcely aware of him. Black sat huddled and shivering, like a crow, with the long black tresses of hair streaked unnoticed across his face. His eyes, deep-set and almost invisible, gazed fixedly through the smoke and his lips moved as he mumbled softly to himself. He had walked slowly, like a man asleep, from the scene of slaughter, carrying his weapons and a bloody haunch of meat, and now to the black tatters that coiled soddenly about his white limbs there was added a redness of blood; a wounded crow, Harib thought, close to death. In spite of his dislike he felt pity for the wretched figure, but above all he felt fear. Eland, tattered and dishevelled as Black, part naked and with bare feet, seemed to glow like a yellow flower in a shaft of sunlight. He had stared worriedly at Black's face for a long while and then, sensing Harib's eyes upon him, he had looked up to meet them and then looked sadly away.

Eland was making no effort to move, so Harib cut as much meat as they could carry. He made a rough bag of plaited vine while Eland helped to carry the meat back from where the buffalo and the the blood of their companions lay. Black seemed unable to stir, so they left him, knowing that they could do nothing. Once, when a far-off trumpeting told of elephants, he had started and looked wildly about him, whimpering like an animal, but the fever that had captured his mind and body responded to nothing else.

It seemed to Harib a strange thing that after all the miles they had travelled, and after all they had suffered, the giants should be so little concerned with the pebbles of their destination. Perhaps already the cost was too high and that no value could compensate for their misfortunes. In the strange half-sign, half-spoken language which they used he had told Eland that the place was no more than a day's journey towards the sea, and towards the way of their escape from the forest. But Eland had only nodded and half smiled and clicked his tongue slowly, as though preoccupied with some private irony of thought. Harib knew that Black could walk and he thought that it would be better to reach their destination at least and then camp for as long as they needed; there was plenty of food. He had even found a wild hive in an old dead yellow-wood stump with more honey in bulging yellow stalactites than they could eat in many days. Besides all this, and given the time for patient stalking, he knew that with his bow he could find monkeys and birds and the little antelopes that tiptoed in delicacy along their mazed, invisible paths. And Harib found himself impatient to be gone. The place where the pebbles lay had been too long in his imagination not to beckon, now that it was so close. He remembered the thrill and pride he had felt as a child when he led his elders to a new honey tree he had found and how nervous he had always been that the tree could somehow have disappeared. He felt a similar sort of excitement now; and beyond the forest lay the great sea where his own people lived, the caves of his childhood, the yellow beaches flooded with sun and the sound of the sea; the warm yellow beaches a world away from the dark forest. The fort and the gaudily clad giants were only a dream and becoming less real with every step closer to his own home. But he thought often of Tassie with her big eyes and the way she walked and laughed, and her image remained diamond bright in his mind, evoking always a mixture of happiness and sorrow, like a good thing passed, never to return.

When at last they picked up their pitiful possessions and helped Black to his feet he felt a surging lift of spirits. He wanted to run and shout; to run away from the forest and from the evil which dogged them. Somehow he felt that at the pebble place the evil spirit of the talisman would be exorcised and he would be free to live again; to be shed of the obligation and responsibility which weighed so heavily upon him was an almost over-whelming desire. But they moved slowly through the rank undergrowth of the river bank, helping Black, detouring sometimes where walled cliffs pummelled the river into a raging torrent and pushing their way through clinging thickets. And the forest looked over them on either side, a trap, marked by the ribbon road of sky that twisted and turned like a river above them.

It was late in the afternoon when Harib knew for certain that the place lay before them. A jagged spine of white rock curved down into the water ahead as they rounded a bend in the river; there was the cold white beach, the buffalo path and on the bank to one side, in a grassy clearing, a charred log like a relic from some past existence. Now he looked with new eyes as he waded through the shallows, and the pebbles were there. He had not noticed before how they spilled out of the cracked white rock to glitter where the water touched them; the rock was crumbly and full of holes and seams like an enormous bad tooth and the pebbles lay thick as fallen flowers. He looked back and called to Eland, smiling and pointing with his finger, and watched as the luminous figure, tall and tattered as a moulting heron, came splashing towards him in little lurching runs with Black reeling at his heels. Harib watched Eland's eyes as he came and they were wide, blue, and his mouth was open with breathing. The eyes were locked to his, as though waiting for the mocking of a taunt, and then slowly, reluctantly in disbelief, his mouth closed grimly to prepare for disappointment as his eyes swivelled down. Time in the forest had ceased; even the river music faded, and Harib saw the giant kneel in the water as though before a powerful chief. He watched hands moving slowly towards the pebbles and then Eland's head turned so that his eyes burned again and his mouth opened slowly and then for the first time, as though the river had come up from the giant's kneeling rags to trickle from his eyes, Harib knew that Eland was expressing his gratitude and he did not know what to do. He laughed. Away in the forest a lourie giggled and croaked. Eland was now smiling and laughing and Black was crawling through the water with his beard awash like an animal swimming towards its goal with hunters behind it. His eyes were wide and he croaked sounds like a hunted creature at the end of its strength. Black clutched at Eland's rags and Harib heard the tearing as though of flesh. He watched the sodden figure rise and stagger, splashing in the water, as Eland's great arm held him, and then as he took the pebble which Eland gave him he grew still and seemed to be pushing it into his eyes and then he bit it with his teeth so white against the black of his beard, and shaking all over, whether in tears or laughter or weakness, Harib could not tell, he sank slowly down to crouch in the soft current with the pebble before him.

As it grew dark the giants moved reluctantly away from the rocky bank that glowed with whiteness against the dark water and the black forest. They brought their weapons across the river and loomed over the fire Harib had made, extending their hands and toasting themselves. Now, once again after many days, Harib heard again their quick guttural talk and he was happy as he grilled the meat for their supper, listening to the splutter and sizzle and the quiet buzzing of the forest and the river. The shadows of the giants cast themselves upon the screen of the forest and the glade of grass glowed like a green sea thing under the light of water. The giants played with the pebbles in the firelight. Eland like a father with good new toys and Black like a child. Eland seemed at last to become first indulgent and then bored, but Black piled wood upon the fire until its flames roared louder than the river and the silent crescendo of the forest. His shadow beat upon the black-green trees with movement and he laughed and danced until the flames waned. He was a devil dancer, possessed and finally deserted so that slowly he sank into a torpor and seemed to sleep. Eland dozed, too, at last, with the red-gold lights of his head and face a halo of sleep, and in the moment when Harib closed his eyes it seemed he was alerted to wakefulness again. Across the glowing heap of the fire, Black in the flicker of an eye had become a standing movement of danger; Harib could only rely upon an infallible instinct to tell him so, but swiftly as his brain moved, there came the roar and flash of a fire weapon. Eland raised on an elbow fell back and rolled sideways to lie still and then the mad, black figure was upon him. Harib saw a blade flash and all his muscles contorted without command to send him bounding over the fire with his spear in his hand. He jammed the falling arc of the blade upon the shaft of his weapon, hearing the swish of wood cut deep, and as the silver needle flashed at him, he ducked and dived into the darkness away from the fire. Now the demented giant stood confused against the red coals, lost, bewildered it seemed, slow; and Harib from the darkness, coldly, deliberately sent all the power of his arm and shoulder into the waiting shaft across the space, thudding into Black's chest, sending him flying down, arms and legs flurrying like a crow's wings in falling flight. But the spear remained pointed to the night sky when all its movement had ceased.

Harib moaned to himself in the terrible silence and kicked the fire into light; he keened in perplexity over the fallen giants, but they were dead, he knew. His spear was lodged in Black's heart, making the giant's face suddenly sad, and Eland had withered under the blast of the fire weapon. He sat on his haunches by the flames, hugging close for comfort with all sleep gone and only the soft humming of his own voice to dispel the ghosts of his fear. When the flames were high the still figures were terrible and awesome in their stillness and their living hairiness; and when only the coals shone the long bodies seemed to move and speak to one another, causing all the forest to shiver with terror. During the long darkness of waiting a leopard coughed close by and while Harib was still turning his head to find the sound, he heard the soft moan of a voice by the fire. As he looked, wide-eyed, Eland's chest heaved and his hand moved to slide down again slowly in a weight of tiredness. Harib gazed in terror at the stricken giant and very slowly in the motion-less glow of the fire his heart reduced the pattern of its frenzied beating. It could only have been imagination that saw the movement of Eland's arm and yet animals had run from the roar of the fire weapon. Yes, it was possible that Eland was still alive. He rose and advanced cautiously, closer and closer until he was standing over the long sprawled body. Tenderly and with reverence almost, he knelt and listened, for it seemed that he could hear breath being drawn, but the river snatched at the sound, drowning it in hopelessness. At Eland's temple, and matted amongst the long yellow hair, blood spread and trickled to form a shiny pool beneath. Now he bent down and held his ear close to the open mouth and sud-denly there was no more doubt; Eland was alive. Harib bounded up with the clutching panic of knowledge that Eland could still die and in a frenzy of purpose he piled wood upon the fire until the blaze turned the glade into a great hall of green and shadow. Using the last tattered remnant of Eland's shirt he washed the blood away to expose a deep groove of a wound that traversed the side of Eland's head just above the top of his ear. He rolled up his sheepskin cloak to make a pillow for the shaggy wounded head and dragged the heavy body gently away from the fire's heat. Now the tenuous flutter of life, moth soft and delicate as a shadow, flickered with the ambience of the flames over Eland's chest and wide muscled shoulders and to Harib, it seemed as if his own eyes must be constantly watchful lest the playful, uncaring spirit should tire and fly away. But the morning came with all its clutter of life: the louries and the chattering monkeys and nearby the piercing cackling of a cock francolin by the stream. Harib felt a moment of anger for the uncaring bird and would have killed him had his bow been handy, not for his meat, but in reprisal. As the lit forest steamed and sparkled and then glowed when the sun struck down upon it over the rim of the hills, Harib tortured himself with the ebb and flow of Eland's pulse. He had no interest in analysing his thoughts, but he knew only that the giant, this giant, his own, must not die or half of him, a newly acquired precious half, would wither and perish also. His thoughts flew over the roof of the forest and across the plains down to where his tribe lived on the shores of the wide lagoon. If Eland should die so that Harib must return empty-handed, a knowledge and a wonder like a new sun would be lost to the Outanqua people, and without the preview of wonder or magic that Eland could bring, lack of knowledge of the giants might prove dangerous, even disastrous. For no words of his, no amount of patient story-telling, could shed more than a glimmer of light upon the wonders that the pale giants had brought to the land, nor of the unconquerable danger that lurked in the fire weapons. War was not even a remote dream where the giants were concerned and who would be mad enough to fight with the bringers of such bounty? There was enough for all; but it was so much more which Harib could not explain even to himself. Perhaps it was in the eyes of the giants, this magic; perhaps in the deep green and blue eyes which had so hypnotised him. Eyes that could see through and reach into a man's head and a voice giving comfort through its sound; even the uncomprehended language seemed somehow fastidiously logical and sometimes warm, but more often, cold and impersonal, a thinking beyond, an overwhelming knowing of all things so that the immediate ones became diluted with so many others. Perhaps the rain and lightning god would have such eyes himself. And always at this point Harib's vision faded. And then he could only see the ribs like his own, rising and falling, the quick breath catching in his own throat and the eyes hidden beneath heavy lids. He groaned with the worry that was his own alone and his envy for the untroubled creatures of the forest became resentment.

He sat up with a start, knowing suddenly that he must take Eland to the healers of his people and wondering why he had not thought of this before. It was such a positive knowledge that he felt happy. There was no other possibility and in a frenzy of activity he began to seek saplings, strong and straight, and coils of strong vine; he paused only to come back to the fire and feed it with wood in spite of the heat of the day and to hear again the laboured breathing. His only immediate contribution to Eland's life lay in the fire and he fed it industriously, willing the flames to transmit somehow their power to the still form.

Before the sun was directly overhead his litter was completed. Two olive bearers, light and yet strong, would support Eland's weight and drag upon the ground. Three feet from Harib's shoulders they would cross, and between was vine, the red-berried wild grape of the forest, to form a hammock and lashings. The top ends of the poles he would take upon his shoulders and the bottom ends would drag upon the ground. At the ground end was a cross spar to which he would tie Eland's feet and the triangle of vine would spread the weight of Eland's body. With patience and great effort he rolled the passive body upon the sprouting, living bier and lashed the wrists and ankles tight and then with a feeling of incompleteness he walked slowly around the fire. The two long weapons and the small one he lashed to the litter; the long ones on either side for balance because they were astonishingly heavy, it was the first time he had consciously held one, and the short one above Eland's head. He collected all the things he had seen Eland use with the weapons and tied them together in the pocket where the small weapon lay; even the long knife was too great a wonder to lose. At last it was only Black who bathed uncaring in the heat of the fire. Tenderly and with a curious ceremony, Harib extracted his spear and then dragged the body through the trees and slid it gently into the stream by the white reef. The water was shallow there, but rains would come soon and with them the torrents of water from above; he went back to the fire. Looking around, loath to leave and yet excited and anxious to be gone, his eyes were drawn down to the spot where Black had lain. There, bright and almost brighter than before because of the blood, lay his own necklace, his reclining eland. Very carefully and slowly he lifted it and then put it around his neck, the thong familiar and comforting, the weight of the pebble cold at first and quickly warm against his chest. Smiling now he turned and lifted the spars and, heaving forward, he started down the buffalo path that would lead him and his burden home.

Through the midday silence that soaked into the forest like a golden sleeping draught of sunlight Harib's breathing and the soft slither of the litter upon dead leaves became the only living sounds. The giant slept on wherever Harib rested; in the deep shadows, wrapped by a shadow of green softness to cover his nakedness or haloed by sunshafts so that the whiteness of his skin and the yellow of his hair blazed dazzlingly alien. And at last when the tree line ended at the end of the day, and the coastal plains sprawled before them, it was as though the forest had given birth to a child; but the child slept uncaring, poised between life and death, and Harib's, fingers trembled with gentleness and concern over the fluttering heartbeats.

In the evening, in the light of the fire, Harib untied the vine thongs where they cut blue and red into wrists and ankles and repaired the litter. He rolled the shaggy head back into comfort and listened with his ear to the heartbeats. He measured his own against those far-off ones of the giant and sat gazing into the bearded face with its big, thin nose and powerfully boned jaw and he missed the eyes long hidden under lids and lashes as soft as those of a seal. And all the powerful muscles were helpless and as weak as moths in a pond.

The stream tinkled. Once a lion roared far away where the eland herds would be and he was quickly aware of the open plains which had released him from the forest. In two more days he would be home. Two days. Perhaps the giant would die tomorrow and the thought again obliterated all concern for the wild night creatures of his childhood life. Harib was tired but his mind raced with activity, soaring over the long difficult haul that lay ahead and then back along the route they had come.

In his imagination he could see the fort quite clearly, with every detail of its wonders winking at him in an incredible variety of colours and shapes. Then the girl Tassie slipped into the picture, as she had so often before, and Harib frowned and shifted his position to push a log-end deeper into the fire; thinking of her always made

80

him nervous or uncomfortable or excited; he found it hard to tell which. Each step nearer home took him further away from her and he was troubled by the thought that he might never see her again.

He flexed his shoulder muscles and sighed heavily. In taking the dead weight of Eland down to the sea he had committed himself to a Herculean task which now, upon reflection, seemed to have lost much of its first revelation of purpose. Then he toyed with the idea of resting for a few days and letting the giant die, and so salving his conscience. Then he remembered that this was the way his people always thought when problems loomed difficult to solve; do nothing at all if possible and the thing would resolve itself in time. What would Eland have done? he wondered. And then he remembered that this was no nebulous exhibit he was bearing; it was Eland and he was suddenly impatient for the dawn and eager to be on his way.

6

Harib struggled with his burden across the plains beneath the mountain range, and his yellow-brown skin, velvet smooth with the microscopic pores of his race, glistened in the sun. It was late afternoon and by now the smell of the sea breeze was full in his nostrils and untainted by the sweet honey-like flavour of the forest. He was pleased to be free of the forest, as always when he left it behind to go back to the sheltering, enveloping ocean, but his day had not been uneventful. Once, soon after leaving the glade, a leg of the litter had snapped and he had been forced to spend valuable time seeking another and fastening it into position. To add to his discomfort, there was fresh lion spoor on the banks of the first stream he crossed and the scent of lion hung heavy in the air. He was thirsty and the elephant road he was following to the sea plunged deep down through walls of brush on either side where it crossed the trickling water; it was no place to be camping even for the space of a rest and a drink, but Eland was moaning and rolling his head and seemed thirsty, too. By propping the litter up against the bank and making a cup of his hands, he managed to scoop up enough water to wet Eland's head and get some of it into his mouth. He was gratified to see the grimy throat convulse with swallowing and there was one miraculous flicker of blue as Eland opened his eyes for a moment. Harib examined the wound, but it was so caked with blood that he could see nothing. Then a lion rumbled with thoughts of its evening kill and at the same time a humming bird with a breast as red as blood droned for an instant above his head. He fingered his hunting charm instinctively and blessed the little bird; then he shouldered his litter and began to heave slowly up the hill.

At the edge of the plain a mixed herd of eland, bontebok and hartebeest were flowing over the red erica veld in a rhythm of dedicated movement. They thundered across his path, raising a cloud of red dust as their drumming hooves hit the gouged earth road which elephant and buffalo had worn to the sea. He stopped to watch them, knowing that a lion and his mate were somewhere, but transfixed with the hunter's wonder and love for their beauty. They poured down into the hollow road and up the other side with backs rocking and rippling in muscular effort. Then there was an explosion which seemed to come sideways out of the dust; a billowing violent draught of movement that shocked and broke the rhythm of the plunging line, scattering it and spewing out the tawny body of a lioness, half above and half under a young hartebeest. Harib watched in silent wonder and admiration. As the dust settled and the herd disappeared and all sound of the thousand hooves receded, the lioness gulped convulsively with her fangs at the throat of the red-brown, feebly kicking antelope until its high hind leg drooped and finally was still. The lioness released her grip and looked up with tongue lolling. She turned her head from left to right and then looked directly at Harib and his strange burden; he could see her sides heaving and for a moment he felt the atavistic dread of the prey animal under the scrutiny of her yellow eyes, but his presence hardly seemed to arouse her curiosity and soon she dropped her head and began to lick the blood from her prize. He gave her all the space she and the rest of her pride might need for their evening feast, but it meant retracing his steps to a place where he could manœuvre his load up the bank, and dragging it through clinging undergrowth in a wide detour until he could once again rejoin the road in safety. By the time the road dipped steeply down to the great river beneath and forest closed in on him again he was exhausted. At least his litter skidded down now almost of its own accord and it was not long before he could lay down his load and drink his fill from the black water.

Eland lay motionless and oblivious, but his breathing seemed steady enough, so Harib adjusted the thongs and massaged his wrists and ankles. He looked up at the steep slope on the other side of the river. Already down in the

85

ravine night shadows were gathering. He watched a pair of louries as they hopped and cawed in an essenhout tree on the opposite bank and began to unsling his bow, but they sailed away in looping flight on their scarlet wings and he flicked the weapon back into position without emotion as he had done so many times before. But his eyes followed their passage over the tree tops and he was aware, for an instant, of the flickering red of wings in a black mirror pool of water.

He was no longer hungry in the ordinary sense, but he knew that he needed food and help with his burden. The shadow seemed to have darkened. There was no question of further movement now. With the reluctance born out of exhaustion his instinct for survival nagged at him to notice the scoured earth of the elephant and buffalo crossing place not twenty yards from where he rested. This was no place to spend the night and even as he made the supreme effort to drag Eland along the fringes of the forest that leaned over the river and captured its water with a sponge of lily and peppermint-scented shrub he knew that the herds were already on their way to drink.

When he was sure that he and Eland were safe he put the palm of his hand on a white boulder and, as surely as though he had seen them, his senses told him that the elephants were moving down the steep hill which would be his route in the morning. For a while now he was to be a captive of the area covered by the carpet of grass under the tree he occupied; the elephants would get on with their business of drinking and move away from the river before it was quite dark. In this immediate area which he had possessed for the night he would kill his supper and sleep and the elephants could even assist him;

for in the soft earth among a patch of ferns, there were the tiny hoofprints of blue buck and to these little blue antelope of the forest, which stood no higher than the lower end of the calf of a man's leg, the elephants were a nuisance; they were noisy and careless in their manner of pushing over trees and were given a wide berth; two hundred elephants grazing over one area could upset the perpetual mating of angry little male buck for days as they were forced out of conquered areas and into new fields, where sharp, diminutive horns would need to rattle again in conflict. Sometimes the angry males would stand defiantly under the oblivious eyes of some massive old bull and snort and whistle and stamp their hooves, which were no bigger than the fat blue ticks on an elephant's ear, and slash lily leaves with their horns in rage, and then when the last ton weight of a branch had swung back behind the last elephant, like a gate closing, believe that they had frightened the big beasts away. It was doubtful whether the elephants knew of the existence of the blue shadows of the shared forest; and perhaps the little shadow creatures forgot how the passing of the elephants gave them feeding for weeks in new shoots and soft grass among the mountainous droppings.

Harib shot a young female as she tripped down the path which was all but undetectable but which she knew as well as the hair tufts on her knees. The arrow pierced her clean through the heart and projected half its length beyond; she somersaulted and lay quivering without a sound among a patch of blue lilies.

He extracted his arrow with satisfaction and dropped the animal on a carpet of grass beside the tree-trunk, then he squatted by the water's edge, washed the arrow head and began to sharpen the bone point on a stone. He ground the blade by feel with light swift strokes, glancing down now and again but scrutinising the scene before him with a trained, interested eye. The place where the elephants would emerge remained in the outer corner of his circle of vision, but he saw also the rock rabbits basking in the last of the sun high up on the cliff opposite him, and the pair of black duck sailing placidly on the inky surface of the stained water and the fish eagle high overhead which told him that the sea was close. He saw the bees moving in and out of a hive halfway up the cliff face that a bee-eating drongo shrike had shown him and he filed the nest away in his memory for another time. He saw the agitation of weaver birds around the closed basket of the nest suspended so carefully on a slender twig out over the water and because it was a challenge to his eyesight he sought and found the camouflaged tree snake at last. He noticed even the human-like droppings of a baboon on a ledge and those of an otter bleached white and containing the crushed fragments of crab shell.

He replaced the arrow in its quiver and scooped up a cupped handful of water to drink and his crouched reflection shivered and scattered in the mirror-bright silver of the sky. Then he remembered Eland's metal cup; he extracted it almost reverently and, scooping water, sat sipping from it, holding it in both hands like a sacred object. He glanced at Eland's closed eyes almost guiltily and then studied his own reflection in the water.

The knowledge that food was at hand had given a sudden lightening to his heart and he forgot that tomorrow would be a gruelling day; even his concern for Eland was fading in the rough embrace of the old ways; the past seemed a dream and he was being drawn back to

88

reality. But Eland was real and the cup was cold and solid to his touch. And even as the lead bull of the herd came swinging in slow majesty down the trail, with its long tusks challenging all before them, he had remembered Eland's needs and was reaching for his skinning blade with one hand and the warm carcass of the antelope with the other. It was blood that might help to sustain Eland's massive frame. The river canyon was utterly still; there would be no scent of blood to alarm the elephants. Harib had paused momentarily as the thought came to him, but one expert slash had severed a vein and the rich fluid as black as the river in the failing light was gushing into the cup. He propped Eland up against the tree, using the litter to support him, and rubbed his wrists and ankles vigorously. Eland moaned and opened his eyes and mouthed unintelligible words. Mixing the blood with a little water, Harib held the cup to his mouth and watched as he drank. A dark trickle flowed through his beard and into the matted hair on his chest. Harib noticed that all the skin of his body where it had faced the full power of the sun had turned a bright pink and this puzzled him for a while; he had thought of the giants as men with red-brown faces and bodies as white as pig lilies and only now it was occurring to him that the sun could actually change the colour of the skins to a darker shade. He had no doubt that in time Eland's skin would be the same colour as his own.

The elephants continued to pour down the trail in a seemingly endless cavalcade of grey and brown, but now, beyond, there were the splintering, cracking sounds of breaking trees and Harib knew that the herd was moving upwards, the way he had come. The explosions of shattered wood were deafening in the otherwise silent forest and he listened in awe, as always, to the sound of the mightiest of all the forest beasts as they fed. By the time the last sounds of the herd had dwindled and died it was dark under the trees by the river's edge, but the dry grass in his pouch and Eland's tinder box had given him a fire which lit the cliff across the river with a ruddy glare. He had skinned the antelope and cooked and eaten so much that his stomach bulged; the remainder he had put into the skin bag he used as a pillow. Presently he began to feel sleepy and one by one as he let his muscles relax, they yielded gratefully until he was borne away into the oblivion of the night.

With light just beginning to show the feathery outline of the top of the river forest beneath, Harib paused in his laborious climb to rest. His muscles ached with effort and his heart pounded in his throat. Before him the trail with its steep sides that rose up far higher than his head, seemed to go on for ever and lending a nightmare quality to his efforts was the ever-present knowledge that this was an elephant and buffalo highway in which he was virtually trapped. Certainly he could not quickly have escaped with the dead weight of Eland and the clumsy litter. He had chosen the early dawn with this thought in mind, but the hill was longer than he had imagined and his progress slower; and now was the time for herds to move.

When he paused to rest he would listen intently as soon as his panting breath allowed, but the silence was broken only by the single ventriloquist note of bush shrike near and far and all around him in a never ending sequence that would last all day. Near the top of the hill

and with a shock of surprise, he met the only other occu-
pant of the road; it was a solitary leopard padding down
to the river and they met head-on around a corner.
Harib's jaw dropped open and the litter fell with a
thump. The leopard stopped dead in his tracks and then,
in one long bound, he was over the bank and away.
Harib smiled and sang softly to himself, shaking his head
in wonderment as he lifted the creaking litter, then he
threw his weight forward and plunged on head down,
with the ground levelling under his feet, until he reached
the top in a final rush.

Behind him the sun was touching the peaks of the
mountain range and before him the scrub-covered rolling
dunes plunged green and undulating towards the sea. The
hippopotamus lake lay a little to his left and away under
the mist beyond the lake was his destination. He started
forward once more in determination and before the sun
had reached its full power he was already past the hippopotamus lake and on his way through a patch of milkwood
forest. He was on familiar ground now in sandy soil
where the colonies of dune moles lived and where
sourfigs flourished and wild garlic and vine tubers; time
and again he stumbled as mole burrows collapsed beneath
his tread, but he had become an automaton, an uncom-
plaining beast of burden, and he staggered on, only
pausing to wipe the trickles of sweat away from his
eyes.

It was on the fringes of the milkwood grove that he
had another surprise meeting. At first he could not
clearly make out what it was; surely not a reclining bushbuck doe; and yet as he drew nearer he saw the white
flag of a tail and then the hooves and then suddenly the
arrow sticking up from the buck's rib cage. He put down

the litter and went forward to investigate. The doe was still warm and he recognised the make of the arrow as surely as though it were one of his own. The sand-deadened sound of men running came to him quite clearly, partly through his ears, partly also through the soles of his feet, and he stood and called loudly through cupped hands. The sounds ceased abruptly. He waited for a moment, then he called again. He was being stalked by his own tribe and he looked about him quickly with a feeling of growing uneasiness that could easily become panic.

'It is I, Harib,' he shouted again and again with the full power of his lungs, knowing that the noise alone would cause the men to pause and wonder. After a while he saw them. They were four, coming cautiously through the trees, peering at him with weapons poised. 'It is I, Harib,' he said again; then recognising the three and the elder with them in a surging of delight, he called their names, 'One-Eye, Dungbeetle, Seacat, Little-Bird-Running-on-the-Beach,' and in a moment they were mingled in a laughing, jumping throng, hugging and shouting and laughing like madmen. Death had always been a troubling thing for the cave-dwellers, a dark shadow that touched the lives of each member of the tribe, spoiling things; and here was Harib who had been dead and gone and now was back and alive again.

The four hunters heard Harib's tale in astonished silence. They peered at Eland and touched him and felt the texture of his beard; they examined the weapons and the tinder box and the cup and the sword; Little-Bird-Running-on-the-Beach, who had only just become a man and whose mind was preoccupied with hunting matters, felt he had missed the best part of the story, so during a small silence he said, 'Tell us again how you caught him,' and Harib had to explain patiently that Eland was not his prisoner but his friend and that he was close to death and should not die. It was all too much to be grasped at once, but Harib was tired and becoming exasperated with the slack-mouthed obtuseness of his companions. They wanted to know whether he could speak and what sort of things he ate and how strong he was and whether there was any risk of his fighting with the cave-dwellers when he was well again. Had Eland heard the flattering and sometimes wildly inaccurate things Harib said about him he would certainly have been surprised at the extent of Harib's admiration and not a little embarrassed.

In an effort to describe the extraordinary fire weapons and with exaggerated ceremony Harib opened one of the powder flasks and poured some of the 'boommaak-goed' in a heap on a nearby log. Then he made a small fire of leaves and twigs with the tinder box while his companions watched every move in curious silence. When the flames were high enough Harib told them to stand well clear and with only the slightest idea of what was likely to happen, they needed no urging; they peered at him and the gunpowder pile from behind trees like a colony of rock rabbits while he held a dry stick over the flames until it showed a red coal. Harib swallowed and tried to hide his nervousness and was glad that he was not being watched too closely. He crawled towards the log and then lay flat and covered his face with his free hand, allowing himself one eye and two fingers to peep through. He took a deep breath and jabbed the glowing point into the powder.

The effect was startling; there was no violent detonation such as he had expected but instead a sound like a lynx spitting and a flash that almost blinded him and a round swirling puff of blue smoke that rose slowly up into the forest canopy. He blinked his eyes in disbelief. In some ways the experiment had been more spectacular than he had imagined but he could not understand about the noise. The others were yarooing and leaping about in delight behind him, so he rose with dignity and said loftily that this was nothing, they would have to wait until the powder was in the weapon to really see its full effect.

The doe, which weighed quite as much as either Dungbeetle or Little Bird, shared the reinforced litter with Eland and his weapons and rapidly now they covered the ground to the sea shelter. When it was evening they reached the beach and in ones and twos they collected curious hangers-on until the party had grown to a straggling, chattering group. The shelter fires winked at them and others came down to meet them for the news had gone on ahead with the shouts of children. And indeed it was the strangest hunting party ever to return to the ancient caves and Harib was the strangest hunter ever to come home.

7

For a day and a night the sea beat very softly upon
Eland, changing its rhythm to the pressure of the tide but
always caressing until its very blueness seemed to have
filled his eyes as they opened at last. But it was the sun
that finally woke him into its golden stupor out of the
dark and green of his long dream and then the hiss of
the waves upon the beach and the dull thunder of the
rock surf rejoiced with its old ally. He lay for a strange
hour flowing back into himself. He felt the sun and
heard the sea. He saw movement near him, but he was

not concerned enough to turn his head. Above him rose the soaring face of a black and speckled cliff cutting the sky in half and there was green, the swaying green of living vegetation dancing and sparkling its broad evergreen leaves to the increasing roar of the sea.

For a while he closed his eyes again and slept and now his dreams were above darkness, for they revelled in soft sand, utterly golden and lovely, warm as the sun itself, and when he awoke the sand and the sun of his dream lay comfortingly beneath his fingers. Very slowly he moved his hands and then after a while his arms and legs, too. It was a great effort and he was conscious of the sound of his own voice deep down in his chest. The sound of a seagull crying floated overhead and then the bird itself slid across the blue wedge of his vision to disappear over the sharp edge of the rock above. Now very gently, as though in apology for the necessity of his awakening, a pain grew inside his head and flowed down into his eyes. A tender force from behind him raised his head and, with only very mild interest, detached and vague he saw his body naked and glowing in a yellow cascade of sunlight. Beyond was a beach white as bone and beyond the beach a white line of breakers fringed the living relentlessness of the sea.

From the sea line a moving thing shimmered into perspective and grew rapidly bringing a new sound with it; Eland watched puzzled and curious with the little lights of memory flashing in his mind as the speck grew to become legs and arms running and shouting over the sand, for the shoulders to reveal themselves stark brown against the white background, and for the face to become a known face, beaming and shouting delight, beckoning as it came. He felt the swirl of hot sand against his thigh as the figure dropped beside him and then with a deep puzzlement he looked up into eyes that were full of tears. Beyond the pain in Eland's head lay nothing but darkness. He saw the mouth open and then, in such a clear boom of sound that the sea was silenced, he saw the man point to himself and heard the voice say 'Harib'. So he smiled and nodded watching the smiles and tears that his nodding brought. Now other faces loomed above and beside him and human sound washed across him to fill his ears and crash again and again upon the barrier where pain lived.

Two days brought a wonderful awakening and with each hour the paralysing weakness of his limbs withdrew while he ate and drank the soft food that was given to him. Always there were voices about him and sometimes laughter and singing. There were shadows that passed across the rock walls and the red glow of flames. There was sun and wind and cold and heat until at last the mist over his eyes disappeared with the pain and he was alive to his surroundings.

Harib spent a good deal of time with him, helping him to walk and preparing his food. The two of them could understand each other more easily and in a more abstract and relatively profound manner than was possible with any of the others. The young woman who often sat with Eland, and who had fed him when his muscles had lain dormant, could communicate with smile and gesture, but the two older ones only giggled or gazed spellbound when he turned his attention to them. By now each member of the tribe had come to gaze into his eyes, egged on by others, and then fled to the back-slapping ribaldry of their fellows. There were close to fifty people who lived permanently in the long complex of a shelter under the overhanging cliff, but many other strange faces had come to look and strange hands to touch gently.

The weapons occupied a special place on a raised shelf at the back of the shelter and Harib presided over them with obvious pride. No one was allowed to touch them and it seemed as if there was never a moment when a little group was not clustered around the place, listening to Harib or gazing in awe and fear.

The shelter faced eastwards across a leafy screen of twisted trees through which a tunnelled path ran down to end in a dramatic circle of beach-white morning sunlight. Looking out over the screen of trees, the expanse of beach swept far away to the right and out of sight behind a towering cliff; to the left a still lagoon caught the waters of a river that ran down a deep tree-grown ravine and fed them into the sea over the sand. At high tide the sea pressed up and the lagoon became green and alive with movement and the swirling and jumping of fish over the whole of its half-mile width. Beyond the lagoon lay isolated rock needles with sand-dunes stark hot and naked where they mounted out of the beach, and softly clothed with green scrub where they stretched further away. Away to the north, wooded hills and mountains turned slowly blue under the long reach of the sun.

As the days passed Eland became less of a curiosity to the cave-dwellers but still apart from them and accorded some special palpable deference that could not easily be defined. The colour of his skin was starkly different among the dust-yellow bodies and he was vastly heavier and taller than any of them, but it was a deeper thing which lay somewhere between his weapons and his eyes, a deification of a sort, an acknowledgment or a suspicion of potential power which might be either good or bad.

Now that he was recovering and aware of his surroundings, his mind probed the reactions of the cave-dwellers: their laughter and amusements, their vexations; their emotions of love and tenderness. None of these things was in any way alien to him and with each day there came a lessening of the lonely waiting for some special form of punishment he had felt to be in store for him. Slowly he allowed himself to believe that the people, to whom he undoubtedly owed his life, required nothing of him in return. He could not understand why he should find this so hard to accept, and partly in guilt and partly in gratitude he tried to make himself useful.

The daily gathering of food was the overwhelming preoccupation about which all other things revolved. Food was the background upon which the simple tapestry of life was woven. Without food there could be nothing, for life itself would cease. And, conversely, when food was plentiful, life could unfold to the full extent of its repertoire, like a desert plant turning its whole intensified chorus of living to the sun when rain has fallen at last. Every morning with the rising sun the men left the shelter, sometimes in small groups and often as a single band. After the men had left, the women would follow, until only the very old people remained and the youngest children.

Eland slept like all the others in a shallow depression in the ground which had been filled with soft-leaved bushes and covered with dry grass. His only covering was a thick soft skin. Harib had given him a skin flap with a thong which he had tied about his waist and he was tolerably comfortable, for it was midsummer and at night the shelter was a blue murmur of body and fire. heat which insulated everything in a womb-like warmth In spite of his frustrated desire to be useful and the almost continuous gnawing of hunger which lived with him, he was content to await developments and as it was obvious that Harib still considered him to be an invalid, he was not too concerned about being relegated in idleness to the cave with the old people and the children.

The shelter stretched under the towering overhanging cliff for at least a hundred yards. In three or four places the cliff curved more steeply inwards to form a cave, but the dwelling place of the tribe was this dusty, hard-tramped, curving terrace some thirty yards wide, roofed by the soaring cliff which leaned over it and protected it. In front there was a mound of empty shells and bone splinters and a fringe of twisted trees with dark green leaves and at intervals paths ran down to the beach, cutting deeply through the shell mound.

After a few days the initial paralysing effect Eland's presence alone had had upon the ten or twelve old people with whom he shared the otherwise deserted shelter began to disappear, and while his every move was still watched archly and his nearness brought a kind of awesome coyness, the pattern of normal life began to continue as before. He tried to make himself as agreeable as possible and found to his surprise that his smiles and laughter brought an immediate response. He clowned for them a little too and pulled faces and one wizened old man went into such paroxysms of wheezy laughter that Eland almost feared for his life. His spluttering and coughing and the toothless expanse of his tiny crinkled face set Eland really laughing too, until the children ran back with their arms only half full of firewood, to see what was happening. As his popularity soared and they discovered his interest in their work, the old people vied with each other to show him their crafts; they were almost pathetically pleased to see his interest and here in the old heart of the tribe he felt the pulse of the tribe's nucleus. The patient borer of stones who ground the last of his life away with the hardwood stick and abrasive sand; the artist who mixed his berry juice and blood and red ochre upon a stone pallet; the shaper of bone awls and arrow and spear heads; the plaiter of grass and vine who made baskets and nets for the capture of game in the forest; the grinder of seeds; the pot-makers, the cooks, the skin-workers; the makers of ornaments; each worked absorbed, at his own pace and to his own satisfaction, wanting nothing but his own respect and a share in the tribe's prosperity; coveting nothing, for there was nothing to desire that could not be obtained except food when food was scarce.

Food flowed into the shelter at sunset when the men and women returned and the children too with their firewood and berries and roots or honeycombs. If the men had been successful their singing would tumble down the gorge in a throbbing rhythm and the women and children would scramble out to meet them, adding the sound of their own voices as they hastened away. A buffalo or an eland was a royal prize, but a burden that required many men and sometimes when the kill was far away, in some inaccessible place, then darkness would fall and the shelter would be hushed without its men and fearful, so that the sound of the sea hissed and whispered unchallenged about the waiting fires. And the women and children would go hungrily to sleep unless the moon had given them a tide low enough to enable them to fill their baskets with shell-fish; and always then there was a troubled excited expectancy. Tomorrow could bring a runner with news of meat and fat and skins, a sudden burgeoning of wealth for all, but always there was the knowledge that some catastrophe could have overtaken the hunters, a clash with enemies, a wounded elephant or a cow with calf, shattering and crushing the forest with rage.

When an able-bodied man or a woman died then a part of the tribe died, so it protected itself and cherished and loved itself, leaving no room for hatred and experiencing all of life through the lives of each individual. They shared everything, for that was the only way. If the hunters brought back only birds and monkeys and rock rabbits or a few fishes and a basket of periwinkles or a clutch of sea bird's eggs or some armsful of roots and honey, these things were carefully divided. They shared their possessions and they shared the women; the women belonged to all the men and in this ultimate brotherhood, the last obstacle to harmony was removed. The common enemies which lurked always close at hand were the hunger of other tribes, the weather and the fangs and claws of the creatures they hunted.

Eland's arrival brought with it two rare natural phenomena, quite apart from the magic of blue eyes and white skin or yellow hair and the shiny metal of his weapons. The first was a savage storm that raged for three days while he lay unconscious and the second was a sudden vicious malady which swept through the tribe like a bush-fire. Only one old woman died from the sickness of coughing and sneezing and the aching of the body passed soon enough, but Harib's stories and the lightning which flashed continuously while the long body lay white and naked in its glare brought a fearful reverence that no one could name or fathom. The storm brought as well a windfall of fish out of an icy current that came from its roaring heart to grip the coastline in swirling fog. The beaches were littered with fishes of every description and for a whole week the tribe lived in luxury on an unearned gift from the sea.

Eland himself, half conscious, had unknowingly gathered the first strength that rekindled the fires of his life from the juice and soft flesh of a fish. Harib had been convinced that Eland's magic kinship with the fire of the sky had created the very conditions of his rebirth, for the fish came at a time when food was scarce. And the rain that followed had extinguished a raging plain fire above the forest, a fire caused by lightning; all the hunters knew that soon the eland and buffalo herds would begin to move across to crop the new shoots as growth began again. As a talisman, Eland unknowingly had the absolute confidence of the tribe and his weapons slept yet unproven.

He spent as much time on the coastline and in the forest as he did studying the intricate techniques of the cave crafts. He learned to distinguish at a glance the edible roots and berries, to set snares, to catch fish with a short line and a gorge hook, to beeline for honey, to dig for clams, to find eggs high up in the cliffs, and each day brought new wonders of discovery until he could not believe he had ever lived before. Day by day, too, he was learning the language of the tribe.

Harib he saw only in the evening and then not every evening, but this was no mere recuperation, it was a carefully programmed tenderfoot tuition, an initiation into the tribe.

During this time, too, the weapons lay untouched and when at last Eland was able to understand from Harib that he should demonstrate their power he realised that he had been expecting such a message. Harib had known that the unlocking of these secret things should not be done lightly and he knew too that the tribe had waited with patience. They were gathered now, a sea of brown bodies and expectant faces; oval faces with pointed chins and high cheekbones, brown-eyed, black peppercorn hair, inscrutable. Some of the women carried babies slung in skin cradles over their backs, some of the men carried spears and others had their bows and quivers across their shoulders.

There was no sound as he lifted the heavy musket and lit the matchcord from a fire and blew on it until the little glowing end showed through a wisp of smoke. The crowd pressed close and then began to fall back and murmur. Very carefully he measured a charge of powder from his flask and then chose a ball and a patch from the pouch. He rammed the ball home and replaced the ramrod. Carefully he filled the touch pan with loose powder, having first cleared the flash hole through to the chamber with a grass stalk. He adjusted the slow match cord in the serpentine and secured it; the weapon was ready. He looked at Harib. Harib gave a command and the crowd fell further back while those behind pushed and craned to see. Eland laid the weapon across the crook of a milkwood branch and aimed at the black lagoon water where it was smooth and unruffled. He pressed the trigger.

The roar of the weapon crashed against the walls of the shelter and fled away up the gorge, echoing and rolling as it went. In the water a white spurt leapt up and disappeared and over the dully gleaming metal of the weapon and about Eland's head like a wreath, blue smoke glowed in the sun and began to drift away.

The shrieking wail of an old woman followed after a detached interval of stunned shock; and then others screamed; the front line of onlookers broke and those behind in the pressure of panic fought to free themselves from they knew not what. The horde scattered yelling and soon there was only a dust cloud to mingle with the powder smoke. Eland and Harib looked at each other in amazement and then Harib began to laugh. He slapped his knee and laughed until the tears ran down his cheeks and until Eland could not help but laugh too, and nothing could have been better designed to allay the fears of the tribe and bring the men slowly back out of their hiding places.

For his own satisfaction Eland fired the other musket once and then the pistol, and the men watched him, flinching at the explosions but whooping with delight and joking with each other. They examined the powder and wondered at the roundness and weight of the lead balls. They waited eagerly for a turn to hold the muskets and gaped at their weight. They kept up a continuous chatter with Harib and every now and again he would falter in his answer and then, with a glance at Eland, give a quick positive reply. The men looked up at the sky and then at Harib. They began to collect their weapons. It was at this moment that Harib became an acknowledged head of the tribe and Eland a kind of super being.

8

Harib and Eland sat together and a little beyond the rest of the party. Dappled with light and shadow, the men of the tribe moved occasionally to send sudden flashes of shine and shimmer amongst the shade green of the trees. They could feel the sun on their legs and thighs but their heads were in shadow. Close by water ran cool and tinkling; a bird pierced the silence with a long needle of a note, tiredly, drugged by the sloth and bee-filled air of the place. Harib lifted the clay pot to his mouth and drank again, letting the water run down his chest in

107

delicious rivulets. He looked about him, knowing it to be well past midday and late, but he was making the pace for Eland and he remembered the long hike up the gorge from the shelter and how Eland's feet had suffered. But he had not complained. At Harib's word the band swung into motion, silent and invisible among the shadows of the trees; a dangerous composite hunting animal with which Eland was as conspicuous and as inept as a child. In every bar of sunlight his skin blazed like the wings of a butterfly and he tripped and stumbled with maddening regularity. Late in the afternoon the pace of the hunters slackened and, when the column stopped, Eland left his musket thankfully against a tree. A slow ripple of excitement and tension flowed down the body of the column and reached Eland through Harib standing close beside him. Harib made the sign of an elephant by drawing his two fingers down and away from his face in a sweeping arc, the curve of an elephant's tusks.

To the cave-dwellers Eland's weapon was an all-powerful implement of magic without limit and it was clear to him now that they would want its killing fire released against the biggest and oldest and most dangerous of all the beasts of their ancestral hunting grounds. The elephant herds that ranged the wide lands were beyond the limits of either spear or arrow; impregnable fortresses of hide that only very rarely succumbed to the wiles of the hunters, through sickness, perhaps, or some cleverly devised trap. They wanted Eland to shoot an elephant and elephants moved close to them now. He could not now explain to them, even if he had wanted to, that for a single hunter with a single musket to kill an elephant was an almost impossible task. The hunters moved aside and glanced back at him; they were notching arrows to their bows; they peered cautiously through the foliage and not a sound passed between them. The long coil of the matchcord had smouldered much of its length away and he adjusted the glowing end in the cocked serpentine with a trembling hand, seeing with relief that the thin wisp of smoke travelled towards him on the faintest breath of forest wind and then knowingly immediately that the hunters would have planned this approach.

Harib peered through the screen of leaves out on to a sloping grove of scrub forest with excitement. In the centre of his vision a bull elephant browsed unconcernedly from the crown of a tree. It reached up languidly with its trunk, swinging massive yellow tusks as it moved and tore down the branches in slow contemptuous disdain. As he watched, it flapped a gigantic ear, setting a branch rocking with a hiss of leaves. Beyond the bull, he counted six others a little way off and half hidden, but it was possible, he knew, that there could be twenty or fifty or a hundred. He beckoned to Eland.

The elephant stood with its right side half turned towards them and with its head only dimly outlined through a veil of leaves. To their right lay a spur of rock rising a foot or two in places from the leaf mould of the ridge, curving and disappearing over the crest. Stunted trees and bush grew up to it and then thinned to give way to the open glade where the elephant stood immediately below. Harib was on his stomach and watching Eland, waiting for him, and with a last look at the priming of his weapon, Eland sank to his knees and then to his side and, stretching his legs out behind, he began to follow, to inch his way along the rocky wall as Harib was doing. With absolute concentration, willing every muscle to stretch and contract in slow motion, lifting and dragging, digging with their toes and elbows, hearing the labouring of their hearts, as the only sound their tortured bodies made, they moved with excruciating slowness and not a rustle nor a snapping twig nor the chink of the musket was loud enough to reach beyond their own ears. Blood began to pound in Eland's head and he was alarmed at the possibility of fainting, so he rested for a moment with his eyes wide and staring at the intricate pattern of a brown leaf that his breath stirred as though there were a gale in the forest. An ant crawled over it as he watched and in some lonely compartment of his mind he was seeing his own proportion of life and death in the quickness of the ant and the leaf already burned with death, having contributed its life to the tree and then cast down and forgotten, and the ant was uncaring; caring nothing that the leaf had been green once and fluttered living in the wind. Nor could the leaf know that the ant would die under the next weight of the giant's knee, nor could the uncaring elephant know that little human giants stalked him with their brains.

Harib stopped and beckoned again and Eland raised his shoulders on the strength of his arms and peeped between the cracks of a broken stone. He suppressed a shudder of excitement and looked again. It was true, the bull elephant stood broadside on and not five musket lengths away from him. It had moved, and now a cow stood beside it with a calf beyond; he could hear their breathing and almost he could hear their hearts, but his own was so loud that there was no way of knowing.

Quietly and infinitely slowly he manœuvred the musket into position, moving back from the little wall so that only the tip of the muzzle rested on the moss-covered cleft of rock. His eye saw the long line of the barrel that knew where the great beast's brain lay and then he gave his eye time and the weapon time and after a while when the elephant seemed frozen in its motion he told his finger to press the trigger. As the roaring weapon pushed his shoulder back, he remembered and delighted in the extra charge of powder he had loaded. He saw the half-real plume of smoke spurt and hang swirling; he saw the great brown animal motionless as a tree, and when the echoes of the shot rang away behind it and it was motionless still, he allowed his heart to leap up, knowing that it must turn and go within a second or else it was stunned to death. But the echoes towered away to the blue mountains and beyond, and slowly, slowly as a boulder beginning to roll down a mountainside, the elephant crumpled upon its great forelegs, let its head sink to the ground and roll crashing upon a tree, splintering and tearing and dusty until all was still again. Away and away the herd rolled and trumpeted, pealing into the silence of the uncaring land, letting the whole forest slip back into peace and silence about the great bulk lying so big and still and forgotten.

The men of the brown skin ran shouting upon the fallen elephant, stabbing it with their spears and cutting into it with their arrows. The forest rang and shook with a new sound as Eland rose like a sleep-walker from the rock ridge, smelling the lethal blue smoke of his weapon, and listening to the hunters as they exulted. Harib came towards him from the mountain of the elephant, and clasped Eland's shoulders, his face was taut and turned up towards the sun, he had dropped his weapons and his arms were half raised as though in celebration of a joint victory. One by one the men of the tribe broke away and came to Eland, following Harib, and only when Eland laughed and stepped across the ridge, shouldering his musket like a king, did the men seize their weapons and run before him chanting as he strode, until the forest was flooded with singing.

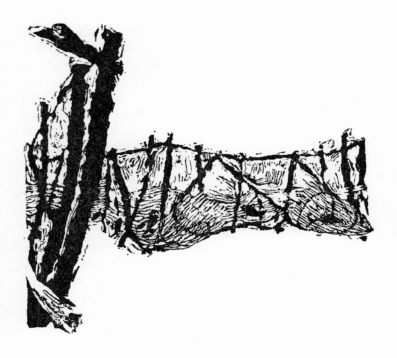

9

The killing of the elephant established Eland and his weapons finally as being all-powerful and quite beyond the understanding of the men and women of the tribe. The day of the elephant became synonymous with Eland's arrival, and time was measured in terms of before or after, a reference needed now, for life was undergoing a change that was based almost entirely upon the availability of food. It had been Eland's sword, too, which had helped to dismember the elephant, and already the blade was wearing thin from constant sharpening.

Like a god, beyond competition with mortal men, he aroused neither envy nor jealousy and only a little fear, and if the tribe had venerated nothing before they had an idol now; for such a being all things were possible. They remembered the storm and the lightning flashes and the great rain. They remembered the elephant falling dead and those who did not were told over and over again. He was a benevolent force from which all good things could come if only it was known how to ask. As the blinding headaches which had assailed him for so long became less frequent, so his strength and full awareness seemed to grow to new proportions. His skin had become brown with sunlight and impervious to it and the soles of his feet had developed a horny coating which enabled him at least to keep up with the other hunters; his hair was yellow from the sun and his beard flowed red as autumn down his chest. He tied his hair behind with a thong to form a kind of pig-tail and when his beard became too long he chopped it off between two stones.

Around his sleeping place, which had become a mani-festation of his presence, there had arisen a separateness and a kind of mysticism. What had begun with branches and then a few stones to keep out breezes was later finished voluntarily by the others in stone and driftwood to form a little room where Eland slept and kept his weapons and a mounting accumulation of things he had adapted for use. Around the cairn had grown a ring of skulls, baboon and antelope and seal, the animals which had fallen to his musket. The building of the cairn was Harib's inspiration, for in his mind's eye he could still dimly see the looming walls and buttresses of the giants' castle. Grass-lined and with skins, the stone room made a comfortable nest and retreat into privacy which Eland found that he craved more than anything. The others slept at a good distance from him, and none of them, not even Harib who was closest, embellished his little sleeping pit with more than the customary bushes and grass. None of them would enter the room except by invitation, but it became little by little a communal talisman which they touched on their way to hunt or to which they added a small pebble as they passed.

The language of the cave people, impossibly complex at first, had slid unobtrusively into focus, but it gave little scope to abstract thought. In minute detail one could describe the progress of a hunt or the movement of a herd of game but the rest was a blanket of vagueness. Eland was in demand as a story-teller. They would crowd around in the evening outside the stone cairn in its rocky corner and build his fire high with flames and listen to his voice as he told them of how they themselves had hunted that day. 'And then Bigbird took his spear, the one he had made before the day of the elephant, and he ran through the grass where it was tall and Lovely Sea Lion ran from the big tree place. . . .' On and on it would go and as he mentioned their names they would smile and shuffle and turn their heads towards the craning faces which seemed to be noticing their friends or relations for the first time.

The place where the shelter lay became full of another summer of beauty and summer sound. The water of the lagoon changed its colour to suit the sun and was in turn tinted by the tides and flushed with the moving pink of flamingoes' wings. The yellow beach beyond flamed and shimmered and then was suddenly mirror cool where the last white feathers of the sea touched and stroked it; within sound of the sea scarlet-winged louries cawed and purred over crimson wild grapes, and the bees, uncaring, built their honey hordes in dead trees, filling the hot sun's breath with a laziness of wine.

Eland revelled in these days; he rejoiced in the muscled excellence of his body and the very sensuousness of food when he was hungry; of cold water from a stream when he was hot and parched with hunting; of the cleansing luxury of the green lagoon at the day's end; of the free pleasures and the dreamless sleep of exhaustion. When he first plunged into the lagoon to wash the sweat from his body after a day in the plains the hunters had stood by watching curiously; water was either for drinking or fishing, not pleasure. Harib was the first to try, and timidly the others followed, and since then it had become a kind of summer ritual which the women joined some-times so that the whole ravine rang with squealing delight. Patiently he taught the bravest of them to swim and again Harib was his best pupil and when they had mastered the still lagoon he took them to the open sea and so it was that the shell-fish foods of long unattainable rocks became theirs for the taking to make the tribe richer still.

While he was twice as strong as the strongest of them there were many skills he found difficult to master. The simple process of fire-making caused his wrists and arms to ache intolerably long before the first wisps of smoke appeared and fire he needed for the functioning of his matchcord musket. While he could run faster than any of them over a short distance, in a marathon of endurance they could jog for mile after mile in swinging, tireless motion that left him far behind.

As stalkers, too, they were incomparable, soundless and swift and invisible. Eland had once watched a

116

hunter stalking a bush antelope in open country and he had marvelled at the skill and patience of the man. The doe had stood feeding two hundred yards away in an open glade. As she lowered her head to graze, the man inched forward towards her, upright and in full view; in the second before she flung up her head to peer at him the hunter froze and the two gazed at each other in utter motionlessness for an interval that seemed never-ending to the hidden watchers. Satisfied at last, the doe lowered her head again and once more the man moved. Time ceased to exist until at last he stood incredibly a few yards from the normally timid creature, able to catch her with his bare hands.

And yet, born hunters as they were, the capturing of game was no easy matter. Pits in the forest dug labori-ously with sticks and stones and bone and woven baskets for dragging out the earth, painstakingly made deep enough to hold a buffalo, these could be bypassed for ever by the herds and become filled with rain, or the sides could collapse from clawing hooves. Bark and vine nets could be ripped to shreds by the flashing white scimitar tusks of wild boar; precious arrows with fine stone heads, hours of work could fly away and be lost for ever in the twilight world of hide and hair and leaf. And men could die as well as buffalo or wild boar.

Eland's weapons remained a marvel and a boon beyond compare. But if his weapons were miraculous his reason-ing ability and his logic and leadership put him far beyond all the wise men the tribe had ever owned; in analysing this quality objectively he had come to the conclusion that the people of the shelter possessed little, if any, imagination. Their improvidence was perhaps the one tangible example of this and in a single decisive step they became through Eland the possessors of salted and smoked food, a never-failing larder for rainy days and a background of survival upon which industry and commerce could be based.

The division of labour, such as it was, already so deeply ingrained into the very soul of the tribe, could hardly bear change, but he had them all toiling joyously for three days to make a lagoon fish trap of stakes and spars. They had planned it first on the dusty floor of the shelter in miniature with small sticks and then cut the bundles of spars and piled them on the lagoon shore and when the spring tides had come and gone the great wings stretched black and proud as a monument over the green water; the trap at the base, an intricate structure of rare precision lit by the flaming moon.

He used his imagination to tell them stories and listened to their own half-myth, half-fact accounts of the feats of long-dead ancestors. Death left them perplexed and fearful and when they sought the answer through Eland he was cautiously evasive, knowing that they would cling with the need for belief to whatever he said, so he told them that those who died lived as the stars in the sky to watch over the living and they were satisfied.

But death saddened Harib and angered him. It seemed pointless; it made all endeavour futile and life itself a mockery. Without imagination the people were happy living for the day—for the deed—and yet without it they were doomed to extinction. But if the death of an individual was final and if nothing lay beyond, then the death of a tribe or a nation or of the world itself and all the creatures in it became of no more consequence than the death of a rock rabbit in a boy's snare.

They buried an old man in the bank below the shelter

118

and placed the flat rock over his head and bent the knees and placed his hands over his face and sent him back to the womb of the earth. And long after the wailing was done, Harib walked alone under the flying moon listening to the tumbling and hissing of the surf on the endless beach, groping in the back avenues of his mind for the reason and answer he knew must be there. But only the night birds answered him and the maze of his thinking was filled only with the sound of the sea. He walked slowly back to the towering slide of rock and shrub where the shelter lay, following the white moonlit path upwards through night-black trees to the lip of the cliff; lit now by a red flush of fires, the crescent platform and the ruddy cliff behind it was a comfortable place of warmth and security. The fire smoke was heavy with a smell of food and outside the stone cairn a young woman knelt to tend a new fire. He paused for a while in the darkness seeing the shadows of moving figures billowing and shrinking against the glowing rock background. A thin tinkle of music reached him and he knew it would be the blind Falling Water strumming his wooden harp of stretched sinews with Dogfish and Flamingo Feather blowing and singing softly through their reed flutes. Far away, somewhere up in the opposite cliff forests, a baboon barked in sudden alarm and a ripple of coughing and grunting swelled and then died into the silence of a leopard's tread. A wind from the sea stirred the bushes beside him and touched his back with a cold finger. He could smell rain in the air. He peered out into the darkness frowning, as if to see Eland more clearly and the old ways of the tribe.

Soon after sunrise Harib knew that Eland had disappeared. They had planned to kill a sea lion that day and as the Bay of the Seals lay many hours distant along the coast they had agreed to leave early. He looked first in the stone cairn and then on the beach. After a while he walked calling in the forested ravine, but only the echoes of his own voice came back. The weapons were there in their corner and the skin foot coverings Eland had made from the belly hide of a buffalo. As the sun rose there was no longer any doubt in Harib's mind that Eland was sick again. Sometimes when the wind blew the long yellow hair away from the wound above his ear, Harib could see the ugly scar, deep and angry and not well healed.

He had seen recently the absentmindedness and the periods of aimless staring into space and he had been alarmed by the flashes of sudden intense activity. Once or twice he found himself wondering how dangerous Eland's condition could be, for his own sake and for the sake of the tribe. He could not imagine life without Eland. For himself he loved the golden-haired giant who was so gentle in spite of all his strength, and for the tribe this new dependence upon alien skills and techniques had become almost a necessity, a new road which could not now be abandoned but which required the guiding hand of a god. He pondered these things as he followed the line of the shore; the high tide had left a clean slate for footprints and the hunters searched on either side of the river that flowed across the sand from the lagoon. Surely he had not set off to return to his own people? But he would never reach the giants' castle alone and Harib knew that if Eland set out on his own towards the land of the western sun he would go with him.

Suddenly again he found the picture of Tassie in his mind and he frowned, for the smiling picture troubled him. He turned at the distant shouting call and then began to trot in the direction of the little group of hunters as they gathered. The tracks were unmistakenly Eland's. The footprints were nearly twice the size of the feet of the shelter people and they led westwards along the beach; in places the lick of a wave had erased them or smudged them to rounded hollows and often they disappeared where rocky spurs sprawled out across the beach and into the sea from the cliffs above. All day the hunters travelled and when night came they camped around their fire, an island of light in the black void of the world.

Harib thought of Eland alone in the blind night of cold southern stars and then his thoughts drifted to the many hunts they had shared. He remembered the bush antelope which had dodged the blast of the fire weapon and then crumpled with his arrow through its neck. Eland had been pleased and full of praise. He remembered the lion they had killed and then he thought of the red fish, the greatest of all the fishes, and how they had carried it back between them while the gulls wheeled above like blossoms whirling in the wind. He remembered the buffalo with the bullet lodged in its head and how it had snorted to its feet and dashed away scattering the hunters and sending Eland flying, only to fall again. They had found the ball below its eye, a hard lump under the skin.

Harib blinked his eyes suddenly as a thought struck him. 'The ball is still in Eland's head,' he said aloud. 'Yes, the ball is stuck in his head.' He slapped his knee. There was a chance that they could remove it.

Old man Puffadder Fang agreed that if this was so and if the wound was on the outside and if the attacker had made the fire weapon kill from the front, then the bullet could perhaps be taken out. Preoccupied with the thought and all its implications, Harib fell asleep at last, while the fire smouldered itself to a pale death in the dawn.

Before the sun had reached its highest point the next day they found Eland unconscious in his tracks under the shadow of Big Hole rock in the bay where so many mussels and oysters grew. He was breathing gently but he had not moved in the sand since he had fallen. While they prepared themselves to carry him back and some of them cooked rock rabbits over a fire and others scavenged in the deep tidal pools of the reef for sea creatures, Harib felt very gently with his little brown fingers around the wound. Old man Puffadder Fang and Big Sea-gull watched anxiously. The round hard lump was unmistakable. Harib smiled and nodded with satisfaction. Then the old man felt and nodded too.

'There is some bone broken around it, I can feel. It is not too deep.' He worked his fingers carefully. 'Yes, we can cut it, but it is dangerous.' As he spoke he gazed up into the sky where a lone black eagle spun gently but he could not see the eagle, for he was very nearly blind.

'First we must take him back,' the old man said at last, moving his hand away from the matted head only after he had stroked the long hair in experimental wonderment. They marvelled at the bulging muscles and at the great weight of the giant and they carried him back to the shelter, back through the summer sounds of deep thickets in a mountainous short cut away from the constant sea. The sea sighing came back slowly as the clamour of bush birds receded and the moon struck whiteness from the powdered ash and lime floor of the shelter. Fires

122

burned to form a welcoming necklace of red jewels around the base of the cliff and they laid Eland in his stone house, waiting for the morning.

Eland awoke to a blaze of sunlight that hurt his eyes as he sat up and looked out over the beach and the sea. When he stood up he felt dizzy and his legs trembled. Supporting himself on the stones of the cairn he moved puzzling towards the smouldering fire where Blue Lily sat working at a coil of clay. Hearing him, she turned and stood up quickly, her little, delicately boned body all suppleness and softness. Against his massive frame she became a brown pixie reaching only to the height of his chest, but she wrapped an arm around him with a gesture of help and led him to the fire.

'You must sit and rest,' she said. 'You have been sick.'

'Sick?' he said, puzzled. 'How long?'

'Three days.'

'Three days,' Eland repeated softly. He sat heavily as though in despair and let his head sink down on to his knees.

'Did I speak in my dreams?' he asked after a while. The girl looked at him half smiling with tenderness or pity in her black eyes, he knew not which.

'You spoke many things, but I could not understand.'

He stood slowly and looked down over the lagoon towards the fish trap.

'They have caught many fishes,' the girl said, rolling the clay between the palms of her hands. 'One very big one, so big. . . .' She stretched her arms out wide. 'A pig nose.'

He could see the men at the trap and small boys sending up sheets of spray as they raced in excitement through the shallow water of the square pen. He sat down again and sighed, knowing that anxiety for himself had eclipsed the interest and sudden excitement he had experienced momentarily.

As he brooded, aware of the girl's glancing eyes but seeing only the quick movements of her hands, he heard Harib's voice and looked up, pleased to find the familiar figure beside him. Harib was still wet and he breathed heavily, smiling with his mouth open.

'You are well again, great Eland?' he asked anxiously, squatting by the fire. Eland nodded and twisted his face into a grin. There was silence for a moment broken only by Harib's breathing. 'The trap is good today,' Harib said at last, 'and yesterday too.'

Eland nodded. 'The girl has told me, I am glad. Pig nose?'

'Many, many,' Harib said. Again there was silence.

'Did I go away from this place?' Eland asked.

Harib flicked drops of water from his upper arms with swift brushes of his fingers. 'We spent much time searching for you,' he said. 'We found you by Big Hole rock, on the sand.'

Eland looked up swiftly. 'By the Big Hole rock? So far?' He screwed up his eyes as a sudden stab of pain all but blinded him and rose to hide from Harib. As he reached his full height a curtain of darkness dropped over him, blanking out light, sound and sensation. He fell heavily at Harib's feet. Harib and Blue Lily struggled to lift him and at Harib's shout three others ran to help. To a small boy he said, 'Quickly, run to Old Man Puffadder Fang; tell him to come; he is at the fish trap.'

The sliver of rock crystal in the old man's fingers sparkled like water in the sun and then glowed white as rain as he moved it into the shade over the wound in

124

Eland's head. Harib watched intently. He saw the searching fingers touch and then open to form a cleft; the old man blew a few strands of hair away, then the blade swept between the fingers in one smooth incision and as the fingers moved Harib could see black blood with only a thin trickle of red dripping on to Eland's ear. Very carefully Puffadder Fang began to scrape the jellied blood away with a piece of polished bone and no one spoke or moved. Now he felt again with his fingers in the wound itself.

The old man nodded. 'It is here,' he said. He raised the little red and black ball and peered at it closely, then he sniffed it. He grunted in satisfaction and all eyes followed as he placed it on a skin beside the still form. He reached into a clay pot and scooped up a handful of dark brown dripping stuff that looked like crushed leaves and herbs in a dark red liquid. A pungent smell of spice and aniseed and peppermint arose. The old man packed the poultice carefully over the wound, turning Eland's head so that the juice flowed down like blood into his hair and over his eyelids on to the ground. At last he sat back satisfied and all the bystanders looked at one another and examined the ball and went slowly away in silence, looking back as though loath to leave and having nowhere to go. Only Blue Lily remained and Harib and when night came up the valley, slowly, tired from the boisterous sea, Blue Lily sat alone in the light of her golden fire circle, listening to the now more normal breathing of the sleeping giant.

As the night grew in stature, sound by sound, fire by fire, so the gathering men and women came to squat for a while and watch the still face before drifting away to their own fires.

Darkness cascaded in a cold curtain beyond the terrace; a bottle bird thrilled the whole valley with the cool liquid of his singing and a shiver of winter blew in across the mist of breaking water on the beach. The flames of the fire waved and Blue Lily closed her eyes as a cloud of smoke swirled about her. When she opened them Harib was standing beside her looking down at the brick-red face under the golden canopy of hair, the face so still and composed, the dark seal skin beneath, so alien, the living giant so far away. He squatted beside her and after a while, without speaking, he lay down to sleep, and Blue Lily curled up at last like a cat among her skins, leaving the night alone and all its soft sounds gathering and twittering and humming, mending the torn meshes of day, waiting for the storm. And in the night, as a black wind sent its first raindrops flurrying into the shelter, Eland groaned and moved and began to awake.

10

The Outanqua tribe had a history which reached further
back into antiquity than any of the elders could guess.
The enormous mounds of shell and bone debris around
the shelter bore some testimony to this and there were
legends and strange myths and stories which had become
blurred with distortion, until they were meaningless
tangles to which the people clung without knowing
why. But the Outanquas knew that to the north-west,
over the purple mountains and to the west, there lay the
great cattle and sheep herds of their nomad compatriots

and that scattered between them like bands of predatory animals were the Bushmen, claiming ancestry with no one, caring nothing and seeking only food.

It was known to the elders that beyond, to the east, were others of the yellow-skinned nation, but beyond these far-flung tribes lay the fearful regions of superstition and dread. It had been said that this north-eastern land was a place of constant fires, a place of smoke and flame and that the people who inhabited it had skins which were burned as black as the charcoal of a cooking fire. Of all the tribe, only Harib had ever seen such men, but Eland's coming had lent substance to his stories, for if there could be people such as Eland was with skin as white as sea sand and hair the colour of bitou flowers, then there could as easily be black ones who killed for sport and ate the flesh of their victims.

The Outanquas had never possessed cattle or sheep for they were hunters and gatherers of food from the forests and the sea. They were proud of their abilities and felt no envy for the richer tribes. It was simply a fact that they lived on a rich coast and had no need to move; fate had been kind to them. They were glad that they were the most favoured of the Hottentot tribes, but that their yellow-skinned nation had existed for thousands of years in undisputed ownership of all the sprawling miles of southern Africa they neither knew nor cared. And they would go on for ever.

The ship out on the horizon crept imperceptibly westwards. And on the cliff top Harib and Eland rested to follow her with their eyes for a while. Faintly still they could hear the sound of singing from the shelter far below. Harib's thoughts flew in exultation like whirling birds on a wind. But the singing was twisting a sadness from

Eland that filled his eyes and tapped at his throat like the beat of the sea. Thin and taut as a bowstring the keening lulled him and cut with emotion across the cold reason of his mind and the motionless ship hung in torment as waves of nostalgia swept over him, threatening to drown him or drag him in two. The womb-soft sun lulled him and the singing cried to him, but feebly, in pity, knowing nothing could win but the overwhelming mind. And so at last, with the farewell music of the Outanquas ringing sadly as a dirge in his ears and the great cliffs, pile upon pile, red, stark, creamed by the sea below, shouting away into the mist-drenched distance, Eland turned, and Harib, rising at once, caught his friend's eyes for an instant in silence and then pushed his way into the yellow shrubbery of the overgrown path; Eland followed.

For a little while after they had gone the yellow fronds of a sugar bush swung and then settled into their wind motion again. A rock lizard with a purple head scurried back to its basking place, to fix the vanishing ship with its piercing stare and then freeze into the lichen covered stone. A long-beaked sugar bird, scarlet and blue, blue and scarlet as the sun and the sea, fluttered over a red erica bush and became invisible. The ship disappeared. The singing died. The long, long stone age adolescence of the Outanquas had ended at last and in its heart the tribe cradled the new men and women who would carry it westwards towards the sun and the sails.

Both Eland and Harib thought of these things in their own way as they went, but in Harib's mind there was no doubt that the old ancestral heroes of the Outanquas had been wise and good and had chosen their instrument well; he knew also that now and for ever the Hottentots and the white giants would be brothers, sharing and loving the broad temperate miles of the southern land, and where the giants led he for one would follow.

By the end of the day Harib and Eland had covered many miles. They had passed the four other Outanqua settlements which lay across the Blackwater river and reached the fringes of the great Tzitzikamma forest. Their course had taken them first along the borders of the sea, sometimes upon high cliff tops and often down among sea-stained rocks and booming spray-filled caverns; they had crossed the estuary mud-flats of the little Blackwater river where yellow-billed wild duck and geese and flocks of curlew tumbled and soared in thousands at their intrusion, and they had climbed the heather-covered slopes of the escarpment above the rivers of Bitous and N'Tokamma. To reach K'nisna, the lagoon like a little sea in the very heart of the Outanqua country, they would cut through the forest using elephant trails that Harib knew, for the route along the coast was a hunting and fishing one and would be many times longer. Harib was aware suddenly of his own sense of urgency, and Eland too was in a hurry.

They camped by the wall of the forest and made a fire that lit the utter blackness of their little clearing with drying heat. Dampness rained softly down outside their circle of light and the now completely familiar scents of saclen, herel and golinseb lingered about them like a greeting. The night was filled with soft sound and not one of the subtle chinks or squeals or grunts was not immediately a whole clear scene to both of them; whether an eland bull gathering his herd on the plains

130

or a sounder of pigs setting out for the night or a monkey scolding her young or the tiny urgent voices of crickets and frogs and mice.

The Outanqua tribes they had passed had pressed upon them a hoard of food and the ululations of the women and the greetings of the men were now again clearly in their ears as sound gave way to sight in the imaginings of the night mind. It was known to all of the people that Eland and Harib were going back to the house of the giants and already in each cave or shelter or forest men were making plans to follow, while the women laughed brazenly and spoke loud enough for the men to hear, of soft clothing and shiny things and strange food.

Looking at Eland by the light of their fire, Harib was once more aware of the latent strength of the enormous man. While Eland's long bronzed body seemed more powerful than before, with muscles that carried no margin of fat, it was his eyes shining with a fire of their own and the quirk of his mouth and the shift of his brow under a wrinkling forehead that Harib was seeing clearly again. If the sparse beard of an elder measured the weight of his experience and mind, then who could say what wisdom belonged to the giant with a beard that touched his very chest and which could surely have reached his feet had not the women cut it and his hair, clamouring for the red tresses as they fell.

Eland lay on his back with his eyes wide open. He had made a pillow for his head with his hands. Beyond the circle of fire it was cold and yet Harib urinated away from it as Eland did. As he returned to crouch once again, warming his hands, Eland said, 'How far is it to the place of the yellow stones?'

Harib had been expecting the question, perhaps even

hoping for it, and now he knew that the giant was indeed whole. 'From the edge part of the Hesaqua country we can reach it in two days,' he said.

'Then we must go,' Eland said softly. 'I think we must go back again.'

Harib stirred the fire with a toppled log. He was thinking of Tassie. Perhaps she would like some of the pebbles too, otherwise they were of no concern other than the cause of delay and an effort to carry. Harib laughed, 'I thought you had forgotten them.' Then he added, 'It was a long time ago. But we can find them again. We will need skins to carry them.'

In the morning early they entered the forest and emerged on the other side of the ten-mile strip before the sun had reached its zenith. Below them, surrounded by a horse-shoe of hills, the shining waters of the lagoon tapered away into folding valleys and spurs of forest. Beyond the farthest hills they could see the open ocean and where the lagoon and the ocean met the circle of hills was cut by bastioned cliffs, red and ochre coloured, through which a ribbon of water gleamed green and deep and fringed with breakers. Marshy islands and mud-flats stretched away as far as they could see and clumps of deep green forest dotted and fringed the shore.

They descended into the valley by a spur of heather-covered hill, following a faint trail, and found themselves being drawn irresistibly towards a spiral of smoke that emerged from a patch of milkwood beneath them. Beyond the smoke, a herd of elephants browsed unconcerned; Eland counted over a hundred and beyond them a mixed herd of eland and buffalo crawled minutely in a speckled line up towards the far hills. The distance was deceptive, and it was hours later that the smoke which lingered over the wooded thicket was close. By now the hills rose high above them on all sides and grass grew lush under their feet. They smelled old fireplaces before they saw them and passed old encampments where ash-grey thorn bushes formed stockades of cattle verdant greenery.

Eland and Harib looked at each other without speaking. They moved cautiously. Now suddenly there were voices ahead but the afternoon shadows provided long hiding places. Eland watched Harib's face, still and listening.

'They are Outanquas,' Harib said at last in a kind of wonderment. He expelled his breath like a sigh and stepped out into the sun. Hey Outanquas,' he called with something of a smile just touching his white teeth.

A voice beyond the trees answered, 'Is it you, black water, by the sea caves, beyond the marshes Outanqua?'

Harib cupped his hands; he shouted, 'We are here.'

It took many minutes for the lagoon Outanquas to come and Eland was aware again of the great distances which the curious sing-song wail of conversation could cover. He had almost perfected the exact tone himself but not quite. They came trotting into view waving their weapons and each one of the twelve talked at the top of his voice in greeting. Harib did the same. Then they stood and laughed at one another, dancing gently from one foot to the other. Eland stood amongst the shadows and listened intently for the party was fifty yards away and the babel of voices made it difficult to hear. His brain began to collect meaning. He knew somehow that he should remain hidden or at least remote and in the background. Quite near him, a puffadder, having recently shed its skin, lay coiled in a somnambulistic circle of brilliant yellow and black. But the snake was asleep in the sunshine and he paid it no more attention. It had no concept of time, it was lucky.

Time of late had become a constant nagging companion of Eland's and awareness of the passing of time had seemed to open new doors in his mind so that there was always an urgency, a goad, a thinking ahead of the next hour and tomorrow and tomorrow. Of all the things Harib had noticed changed after Eland's recovery, this restlessness was the most noticeable. And the eyes that refocused, to look so far away and beyond, were the windows through which he had seen it first.

Eland waited and still they talked; they rested their weapons, they changed legs but the chatter continued; sometimes they shot quick glances in his direction and pretended that they were looking up at the hills or the sky, and then Eland smiled. He had sat down and was chewing a grass stalk. In the distance almost as far away as the cackling of the bush francolin he could hear singing. He smiled again, for all that he had heard was good. The Hesaquas, it had been said, were living with the Outanquas; he knew this to mean that families of the Hesaqua tribe had married Outanqua women and had come to graze their cattle in peace. It was apparent that Harib's brother was amongst the party of lagoon Outanquas and whether 'brother' meant hunting blood brother or brother from the womb of the same woman, made no difference. He heard that hunters from both the Hesaqua and lagoon Outanqua tribes had journeyed to the fort and returned with wonderful tales.

The band was beginning to come towards him and as he stepped out into the sun the men put down their weapons and began to clap their hands. They danced around him humming and buzzing like bees and Harib joined them but he was grinning so broadly that Eland knew he was joking and enjoying Eland's discomfort and loath to offend his companions all at the same time. They were receiving Eland as though he had been a victorious chief returning, or a mighty king from some other region and it was only when Eland had spoken to them quickly and greeted them that they stopped finally and gazed at him in wondering silence, and whispered amongst themselves.

Harib was as surprised at the reception as Eland was. They followed the singing and jumping group through the trees, gathering other men and women as they went and children joined and then singing started ahead of the procession which by this time, it had indeed become. Harib and Eland kept close together, silent, half excited and half apprehensive. They looked about them in surprise as the classic conical huts of the nomad Hottentots came into view. It was a whole unit of an Hesaqua kraal in the midst of Outanqua country; here too, then, on the outskirts of the kingdom of the cave-dwellers, a metamorphosis was in progress. There were cattle and sheep where no cattle had ever been; there were Hesaquas scattered amongst their Outanqua cousins and everywhere the precious trinkets of the giants were evident in flashing bead necklaces, copper bangles, printed cotton and brightly coloured conical caps. The people were collecting quickly and they all looked at Eland; it was obvious that something was expected of him.

In the clearing in front of the biggest hut sat a man who was large and fat for a Hottentot. He was binding an arrow head, sitting cross-legged in the dust with a shred of leopard skin across his right shoulder. He wore a heavy

135

string of bangles on his arms, some of copper, some of ostrich beads and some of the dried animal gut. On his head was a single string of beads with a green glass pendant that hung over one ear. He was watching Eland but glanced down swiftly each time his thumb clamped hard upon the whipping around the arrow shaft. Harib and Eland stopped in front of him.

'Greetings,' Harib said, raising his hand. 'I know not your name, for I come from the land of the Outanquas across the marsh, but I see you are a chief. Therefore I salute you. Now I wait for you to speak.'

The man laid the arrow shaft aside very slowly. Then he rose. 'I greet you,' he said, and a sigh or a cry went up softly from the many watchers who had by now formed a semicircle around them. He turned towards his hut. 'Come,' he said, 'inside we can speak.'

It was dark inside the conical grass-woven hut, but their eyes adjusted themselves rapidly and smarted only a little from the smoke of the fire that glowed on the swept earth floor in the centre. Eland's head almost touched the roof. There was a single pole in the centre, protected from the fire by a flat stone standing on edge. A quiver of arrows and a bow hung from the pole and apart from a few cooking pots, some rolled-up skins and a litter of bed grass the hut was empty.

'Sit,' the fat chief said, easing himself to the ground. They sat down. As they did so a shadow appeared in the doorway and a stooped figure stepped over the fire and sat opposite them. It was a woman but they could see nothing of her face for a skin cloak covered her head entirely.

The chief grunted and peered at Eland. Then he grinned. 'I know of you,' he said, 'but you do not know

136

me, therefore I will tell you. I am Oringa and these are my people and my cattle. I am Hesaqua.'

'I say greetings to you, Oringa Hesaqua. I see you are a great chief,' Eland said. 'You have many cattle and people. We have nothing as you can see and require nothing except perhaps food and shelter. Soon we shall go again to the place where the stone house is.'

The Hottentot chief's eyes lingered upon each detail of Eland's body and gear.

Since his recovery, Eland had changed in many ways and to some degree this change was manifest in his dress. He no longer wore the necklace of shark's teeth, nor the leather bands about his ankles, nor the bangles of dried gut about his upper arms. The flap of skin he had worn about his waist had become a sewn garment of sealskin which covered the lower half of his body to just below his knees. Over his shoulders he wore a sewn cloak of sealskins which had been worked to softness during many patient hours and which he could fasten with one or two or three thongs as he wished. For his feet he had made sandals of shaved buffalo hide. For the rest, his body was naked and unadorned except for the ever-present fire-lock, a pewter flask containing the last of his powder, a pouch for his bullets made from the scrotum of an eland, and a skin bag which he carried over one shoulder. With his red beard and long yellow hair seeming to add height, he towered two feet above the tallest man in this new mixed, mercantile camp.

Oringa's eyes settled at last upon the firelock that gleamed faintly where it rested against Eland's shoulder. It seemed to Harib that Oringa was lost for words and that curiosity and amazement were bursting through the outward calm he was trying to preserve. 'They named you well,' he said at length. The doorway darkened again as a robed girl entered with three gourds of milk. She placed them on the earth floor beside them and withdrew after a hurried glance at Eland.

They drank the milk with full animal pleasure and the customary compliments Harib knew he should pay were genuine enough.

While the still cowled figure watched from a corner, they spoke of many things. Oringa had never before seen a giant. Some of his people had made the journey to the distant fortress and now his questions were unending. The legends had come alive in a living presence whose size and wisdom at least had not been exaggerated. As the afternoon declined they drank more bowls of the heady milk. In the dark light of many fires with the sound of a sea of frogs and crickets, Eland fired his musket for the chief three times and its echoes stilled the whole misty valley, while its stabbing flames imprinted themselves for ever on the eyes of the watching faces. He had lifted and held at arm's length over his head a log which no two men could lift and now they listened as Oringa's envoys spoke of the fortress and the giants and the real people.

Harib understood and knew that, like a softly turning tide, the presence of the fortress was reaching out to the old, the real people of the southern land and gathering them to itself. No man could hear the stories and see the copper bracelets or the red and blue beads and not be compelled sooner or later to join a caravan of traders or sightseers. There was always tobacco for the visitors and perhaps a glass of the burning arrack and for those who brought cattle or sheep or ivory there were rewards of finery such as no real person had ever dreamed of before.

The giants' appetite for cattle was insatiable. The appetite of the real people for copper and beads or woven fabric was insatiable; tobacco and arrack were becoming a necessity but the stocks of cattle and sheep could not last for ever. The herdsman Hottentots had too long lived the good life of the cattle follower to have remembered how quickly the quagga could hear with its round ears and how swift was the galloping gait of the hartebeest and how marvellous the eyesight of wild geese; the heavens made the rain and the grass grew and the cows made milk and the real people drank the milk. The real people were fortunate and had no need to toil by the sweat of their brows like the Bushmen. They spat upon the Bushmen who were not real people and killed them when they could, for the Bushmen stole as a way of survival. And now some of the Hottentot tribes, in a welter of avarice and improvidence, had sold the last of their cattle and now they leaned upon the giants. They sat in the sun and leaned and did nothing. Sometimes they would carry firewood or help a gardener to fetch his oxen. The men drank the arrack and brandy they could barter and they loved the giants. In the giants' shadows the real people nestled and found a new way to live. The giants were heroes out of some forgotten legend and when a few real people died in the fire, roaring of the giants' weapons, it was just, and when a giant was killed it was just, but there was no war; never a war of great killing; the real people competed for the love of the giants and killed each other and now, for ever, where the giants walked these, their children, would follow.

Dimly Harib was aware that the milk had been poisoned; certainly he was drugged and yet he felt neither resentment nor any desire to get away; he was filled instead with a strange excitement. It seemed that knowledge and understanding of all things were flooding into his mind. Time itself was becoming a floating dream of colour. Luminous globes of pure colour were moving slowly around one another, waiting for him. He was a part of them.

11

Harib tugged at his bonds in silent rage and in the utter blackness of the hut. His head ached and there was a creeping of pain which seemed to start from his ankles. The leather thongs had been tied very tight and he could not feel his feet; he could only just move the fingers of his left hand. As his head cleared he began to remember and now he wondered how much time had passed, for it was certainly dark, darker than the inside of a temporary camping structure could ever be. He struggled and then relaxed exhausted to listen. He could hear nothing. He was dazed and mystified and angry.

It had happened after he and Eland had gone into the chief's hut and many hours must have passed. It dawned on him that he was lucky to be alive at all. He struggled mightily and with a rising feeling of panic, knowing that he could yet die. He could not understand why the camp was so silent; or was he miles away in some deserted place in some old deserted hut? It seemed unlikely. His assailants would not have taken so much trouble; but then even riempie thongs were not discarded lightly; life was cheaper than the excellent and strong thongs that held him so securely. When his head had cleared more, he lay for a time listening, but no human sound reached his ears. He could smell no smoke nor could he hear the faintest snap of a dying fire. The pain in his legs had become a dull ache. After a while in a strange drugged euphoria he slept and awakened and slept for a while again and then at last it began to grow lighter. At first it was the sound of a single hippopotamus which seemed to pierce the dark fog of discomfort and pain; and after a while hyenas wept upon the outskirts of the hut settlement and when it was truly light, grey as a shell, a lion grunted and set the frogs speaking to one another; cold seeped up from a mist where crickets dwelt in the damp grasses of the early morning; they tinkled and twanged so much that the frogs became jealous and blew their throats up and became louder and at last the sun came and after a while sound faded under its benevolence; warm and peaceful, a night survived, another day to live as only the mist and the dew died.

Harib wrestled with his bonds and shivered in the damp cold. He was alone. Within a few seconds he had seen the inside of the hut and the entrance with its white light slyly as always peering at the dawn and by the time the sun itself had cast a new gleam upon the inside walls, he had started to roll himself towards the low doorway. Outside it was cold. Four other huts stood silent in the clearing and a trio of doves pecked at the earth not far from him. The chief's hut was dark and silent. Harib rolled towards it. With each turn the doorway hole came closer and at last he was able to see inside. For a time it was only blackness that he could see and then he called loudly in desperation for Eland and the blurred bundle inside stirred. There was a swift series of movements and Eland came out blinking, on hands and knees through the opening. He staggered to his feet holding his head and all but tripped over Harib. He sat down beside him with a groan, shaking his head, and cursing softly. After a while he focused his eyes on Harib's anxious upturned face and began to grope in his pouch for the sword tip he used as a knife. He cut the leather thongs.

It was many minutes before Harib could stand and Eland helped to massage his legs and arms. The camp was deserted. Harib searched angrily for his weapons but they were gone. Gone too was Eland's musket with the powder flask and the last of the lead bullets. Because of the nausea Eland felt, the loss did not alarm him at first and later on, after the initial shock of being parted with the weapon that had become almost an extension of himself, he reflected and only now allowed himself to acknowledge that the life of the musket was nearing its end. In the flask there was hardly enough powder to fill the palm of his hand and the bullet pouch contained exactly ten balls, each one of which had been fired before and dug from the carcass of a hunted animal and rolled to roundness for use once more. The barrel had become worn and the serpentine mechanism rattled irreparably. He remembered how the explosion of the other musket had almost cost him a finger.

But without weapons and men an expedition to the river of gold would be dangerous and futile. It was enough that many hundreds of miles lay between them and the castle in the west and Eland was being drawn back to his own kind with an undeniable urgency. Now his last responsibility had been lifted from him and now he was almost glad of the reprieve which made survival the final challenge.

Their first action was to set a battery of snares for small game; between them they had twelve sinew snares strong enough to hold the pigmy blue antelope but intended for bush francolin and partridges and pigeons. They set them carefully among the antelope runs and francolin dusting places on the fringes of the olive and milkwood forests, Harib taking one spur and Eland the other, and met again at the deserted camp with armfuls of straight olive stems to be trimmed and shaped for bows. While the area had already been scoured for edible roots and bulbs, they found a few; they also brought back a tortoise and a dune mole which Eland had been lucky enough to seize from the top of his burrow.

Before midday they were rewarded with the bleating cries of a blue antelope in one of the closer snares and they raced like boys to catch the tiny animal, laughing and shouting as they went. There was food enough in this place and water and firewood. But their nausea was slow in passing, threatening to surge back when it seemed to have gone completely and by late afternoon Eland was suffering badly. They were sitting by their fire and Eland was cursing the pain in his stomach and rocking from side to side.

Harib, who had been watching him, got to his feet suddenly and, crossing to the chief's hut, disappeared inside it. When he emerged again he carried in his hand a piece of brown fungus and squatted down beside Eland, looking at him and then at the fungus in turn, as though weighing a problem in his mind. He nodded at last and Eland, seeing his upturned hand for the first time, reached for the fungus, smelt it and looked questioningly at him.

'It is this the woman put in the milk, I am sure,' he said. 'It is poisonous and can make you sleep and dream.'

Eland groaned and grimaced, holding his stomach. He muttered curses under his breath while Harib clicked his tongue and shook his head in sympathy and disapproval. He felt vaguely responsible and embarrassed by this act of one of the real people and particularly with Eland involved. Did they not know who he was? Even the Hesaquas, independent and arrogant as they were, could hardly be so casual. Harib was mindful though of the fact that they had not been killed and he knew that he owed his life to Eland's presence. He examined the fungus carefully. He knew it as a rare growth that could some-times be found on one of the less conspicuous forest trees. It was much sought after by the magic healers and, in small doses, could produce a brilliant kaleidoscope of hallucinations. But it was poisonous. In large enough quantities it was lethal, and Harib had heard that the illness would recur again and again unless regular but ever decreasing doses of the stuff were taken. He told Eland all he knew of the fungus.

It took much heart-searching, as well as ever intensify-ing pain, before they could persuade themselves to eat small pieces of it and, even as Eland chewed, his better judgment accused him of folly; repeated doses of the same poison to cure the poisoning seemed against all logic and the belief very likely had its origin in a witches' myth, a preservation of esoteric secrets from the rest of the tribe; but incredibly, and to his great relief, Eland found soon after the sun had gone down over the hills that the pain was lessening; his vomiting ceased and a glorious tingling of sleep began to creep and sing through every muscle and bone in his body. Beside him, Harib lay very silently asleep.

The sound of a splintering bone shocked Harib awake. He lay in the half-light with his eyes wide open, shivering with cold and an utterly intangible fearfulness. His heart beat wildly and the memory of a dream, terrifyingly alien, still flirted with his consciousness. A hyena loomed over him against the white sky as big as a lion. He scrambled to his feet yelling and the beast bounded away into the shadows. He stood swaying on his feet, detaching himself from the night, thinking of how a hyena could take a sleeping man's face away with one bite and all the while the dream was speeding into the realms of fantasy and remoteness. Now was real. The day was coming. He lived.

He thought ruefully of the missing tinder box. Then he searched for his sticks and found them and began to set about making a fire, but he was slow in his actions, fumbling; and snatches of the dream kept slipping into his mind causing him to stop and look away into the distance, all tasks forgotten. He shook his head and began to spin the hardwood stick in practised palms. Eland slept beside him and the dawn crept nearer.

When the little pile of dry grasses began to glow he

knelt down with his head close to the ground and blew a small feather of flame into being. He fed it with handfuls of dry grass and twigs, pouring the fuel in an accurately controlled trickle until there was a glow of red to accentuate the soft white and mauve around him and the sleeping Eland. He stared at Eland's face, now so bronzed and strong in the stark light. He could see the scar where the ball had lodged and the scar on his right cheek where the razor tip of a boar's tusk had grazed in a flash of dangerous white. The long red beard had in it glints of copper and gold like the metals which these strange giants sought. Eland's chest rose and fell and his teeth gleamed between open lips. He felt again the strange mixture of emotion and compassion he had so long felt for Eland. He had suffered much. What drove him, he wondered; what alien forces drummed and urged inside his head? He thought of all the names by which his own tribe had referred to Eland, hero, provider, big head, destroyer of the old ways, giver of new things, teacher, law-maker, thinker, leader, hurry to do things, no sitting in the sun, look beyond tomorrow, and they were not all complimentary or without cynical humour. He turned to wake him as the hyenas pealed again far away, at the edge of the forest.

Because they needed time to make weapons, and because it was possible that the Hesaquas might return to their old camp, Harib and Eland retired to a place some miles up the valley where the broad lagoon narrowed to a ribbon of black river water. It took them nearly all day to reach the new camp, for they moved cautiously, not anxious to risk a meeting with their strange enemies. They were unarmed and still weak from the effects of the fungus.

With the terror of the dream still with him in almost nostalgically painful glimpses, Harib was quite determined that he would not touch the stuff again. They had hardly debated the matter and it was clear to Harib that Eland too had found the experience unnerving. He had tried to tell Eland of his dream and failed. Eland had laughed at his animated descriptions, which caused him to clown and mime even more. He was always happy to make Eland laugh but in fact his mind and memory and mouth could not correlate the dream. After a while it seemed to become funny and finally the terror was gone. Later Eland had said, 'The animals upon which you rode in the dream, were they oxen?' And in a second he could smell the dust of that distant country. He had tried to describe the animals and finally Eland had said, 'Have I told you of animals upon which men can ride?' And when Harib shook his head Eland had seemed thoughtful and become silent.

They set their snares again that evening in a spur of scrub forest, criss-crossed with the almost invisible paths of bluebuck. The tiny lanes, blurred by a soft, constant rain of dead leaves, threaded their way through fern bowers and under twisted boughs and to the unpractised eye they would be as difficult to detect as the pygmy antelope which used them. The little buck flitting in and out of the forest shadow blending their slate blue with the hazy purple background were good meat, but they were acutely wary and moved soundlessly on their delicate hooves. But like the grey monkeys and the scarlet-winged louries of the forest they were inquisitive and many hundreds of them had fallen to

148

Harib's bow as he called them to him with soft sounds from a camouflage of immobility. Without a bow and good arrows Harib was handicapped and uncomfortable, knowing how much he had come to rely upon Eland's gun.

Because they were hungry and impatient they agreed to drive the section of forest in which their snares were laid and so, armed with dry sticks which they tapped softly together as they moved, they advanced from behind towards the apex of a triangle ending back at the river. In the forest the antelope listened to the faint foreign clicking of the sticks. Some listened longer than others, their ears twitching, before springing away with shrill, hissing whistles of alarm to vanish down the trails on imperceptably tapping feet. Some slipped away beyond the approaching sound but two ran the snares taut and sent shivers of alarm through the forest and over the river with their strangled bleating. Harib and Eland arrived almost simultaneously and quickly killed the struggling animals. Across the river a herd of eland, high horned, massive and white against a green background, began to move away and from the edge of the forest a bull elephant gazed at the two man shapes in frozen curiosity.

Sitting by their fire, Harib and Eland ate and planned the manufacture of their weapons of which the two small animals formed now the basic corner stone from which the other necessary materials must come. They were pleased with their catch and blessed their good fortune. For the strings of their bows they would need the tough sinews of a bush buck and to snare a full-grown bush buck that could weigh more than Harib, they would need new snares, stronger than the light ones they carried, snares rolled and knotted from the skins of the blue buck. They would need bush buck hide for binding and bones for certain arrow heads. For the rest, Harib had already collected waterworn boulders from the river gravels and a stone anvil and before the sun was down he had begun to strike the flakes he would need, while Eland, shaving and tensioning arrows and bowsticks, watched the unfolding of the ancient craft in fascination.

The next day they caught two rock rabbits and another blue antelope and then their luck seemed to run out. They had caught a bushbuck doe in a snare set higher up the valley and as they burst through the undergrowth panting from their furious haste, she had whirled in a last desperate bid for freedom, snapped the thong around a hind leg and was gone in an instant. Shortly afterwards it began to rain hard and three days later it was raining still. But early in the morning, after the rain had stopped they killed the buck they needed in the snare that they had laid with such great care. He was an old ram with white tipped horns the length of Harib's forearm and a shaggy mane of hair from chin to deep chest. He was food for many days. They felt that they knew him, having glimpsed him once, a blur of white tail and bars and spots stark against the black hide but more palpably, having known his spoor and learnt his ways in the beaten territory he commanded; the deep spoor in the earth of the sodden forest, the branch against which he rubbed his neck, the place to which he would come when the rain had stopped. And now they shaped and finished their weapons and looked across the river and across the country of the Hesaquas. It would take them fifteen days to reach the fort.

12

They feared two things: the old enemy hunger and a meeting with Oringa and his Hesaqua band. With the fire weapons, Harib would have chosen the direct overland route across the plains and through the game herds below the forested mountains. The three days of deluge had been the rains which ushered in the winter and there would be more rain to come. Another full moon would bring the cold and then frost would encrust the plains at night and bring misery to sleeping men. Suddenly, he missed the fire weapons very much. After the rain, the plains would be a fine grazing ground for game. It was a pity. And he knew that Oringa would have taken the coastal route, touching the watering places and only cutting inland for the sake of his cattle herds.

They swam the river and went slowly up the hills beyond. From the top, looking back they could see the whole, vast amphitheatre of the lagoon. The towering headlands in the distance with the lines of breaking water that were the gates to the open sea. The marshy islands, the mud-flats, the fringes of forest, the horseshoe of hills and then the tapering ribbon of river immediately beneath them. Harib was chewing his lips and rubbing his chin with a finger as he gazed across the dawn-covered expanse of water. Aware at once of Eland's eyes upon him he turned and smiled selfconsciously. He stabbed at the scene with his spear. 'Perhaps we will never see this country again.'

Eland raised one muscled shoulder slightly, embarrassed, for this was unlike Harib. He said, 'You are free, this is your country, it is your choice.'

There was a silence as they looked out and towards the sea. Then Eland said, 'You will have it always, this place, it will be inside you.'

Harib laughed. 'You always have words.'

'Sometimes my words are true, Harib,' Eland said. 'I wish you well. You and all your people. For I owe you my life and I am grateful.'

Harib's eyes were turned to the mountain fringe in the north but a pulse beat in his neck, a soft shadow fed by the rising sun, the light silhouetting his ageless face. Below them in the valley a bush francolin called. Eland framed the words carefully, 'I shall tell them we found no gold.' He paused and Harib nodded slowly. 'Shall I tell them we found nothing?'

Harib turned his head and looked at Eland. 'It is good,' he said. 'That is good, tell them we found nothing.'

The sun was touching the tops of the mountains, each one like a beacon of light, a signal, marching westwards, warning or leading until the whole range glowed in a line of fire stretching away under arching clouds. A new valley lay below them and a new river. They turned away and went down together, laughing as though they shared a great secret.

The dune country slipped away behind them and they fared well on its tortoises and moles, its small red antelope and its wild onions. They lost two good arrows in a buffalo calf and caught a tufted-eared lynx in a snare. When they had crossed the third river they turned toward the coast and a change of diet. They crossed long beaches of yellow sand and around their night fires they ate mussels and octopus and then for many nights the rich meat of a sea lion. The country was strangely deserted. Even the coastal shelters were unoccupied and not one human footprint could they find on any of the long beaches. In one of the overhanging rock shelters Harib found a plaited fishing line with a good bone gorge hook but the line was rotten and broke easily. This was a disappointment. They kept the hook and speculated upon how much more game they would need to give them a sufficient length of sinew. But a fat rock fish would only have been a luxury, for of shellfish, rock rabbits, and sea birds they had more than enough.

Of all the animals which sustained them, the ubiquitous rock rabbits were the easiest to catch. Harib shot them with unerring accuracy. They would peer out from their rock lairs and then, unable to resist the sun, scamper up to bask on boulder or ledge, round bundles of unsuspecting fur waiting for Harib's arrow. Eland was a poor performer with his bow and could not resist clowning for Harib's benefit. Harib found his antics amusing and would stamp his foot and stagger about with a silent laughter when Eland began one of his elaborate stalks, buttocks high in the air and nose to grass. But Eland devised a trick of his own for catching gulls which impressed Harib. He used the short lengths of sinew and some cord made of thin leather strips and baited the hook with scraps of meat. Having anchored the end, he caught nearly every gull which swallowed his bait.

At the end of twelve days they came to an estuary deep and churning, half a mile wide, the water muddy from rain on the inland plains. There was no thought of swimming this brown, dangerous torrent of mixed salt and fresh water and the thought of sharks was another deterrent so they followed the bank of the river for half a day northwards until the stream narrowed and gave them a place to cross. But it was growing dark and they decided to wait until morning.

The night covered them slowly with a carpet of brilliant stars and a dusting of dew. They could hear the chuckling of the river below them and the many voices of frogs and crickets. In the distance it seemed there was a pounding of white crested breakers. The plains above them were silent; for this was the hour of danger; only a nightjar rose and fell on the circles of his own wailing cry and the soft flutter of his wings.

Harib was lying beside the fire with his hands cradling the back of his head and gazing up into the darkness.

'The night bird is saying that the cold comes soon and that he will fly away over the mountains.'

Eland did not reply at once. Then he said, 'Soon it will be cold.'

For a while they lay listening to the soft sounds beyond their fire.

'Four days now, Harib?' Eland asked.

'Four days, perhaps five, not more.'

For a long time they neither stirred nor spoke. Each thought that the other was asleep and indeed at all the camp fires along the way and at so many in the past, stretching back it seemed into the very beginning, they had always fallen asleep quickly, the deep sleep of physical exhaustion. Eland had been about to say, 'How will it be with you?' and he had meant, 'Will you stay at the fort? Do you think you can stay at the fort for ever? How will you fare? Whose tribe will you join? Will we become enemies? How can I repay you?' Instead he grunted and rolled over on to his side to face the fire and Harib. He said at last, as casually as he could, 'When we reach the fort, soon after, I will go away over the sea to my own country.'

Harib turned his head sideways. 'I know this,' he said, 'It is best.' Yes, Harib knew. He understood. It was best.

Eland felt a weight of responsibility and indecision fall from him. Now his breath began to come quicker and he knew a tingling of excitement. That which he had secretly longed for in his inner loneliness; that which was as much a part of him as the colour and texture of his hair. That living stream of a culture linked to the stream of his blood by ties too old to break was to comfort and vex and perhaps destroy him. But he could not live without it for ever. He had not permitted himself to believe that he would ever know it again. Now his heart was beating it out; make haste, make haste. The crackle and drumming of canvas, the exhilaration of a ship in motion, the wind in his face; hasten away from the idyll which was doomed to die. Away from the smugness of the fort, the blind, avaricious, smugness of the fort at the end of the world. Away from meaningless bibles, from bigotry, from prejudice. He saw it all clearly and now he was beyond it; nearer the truth. The fort could neither contain him nor sustain him again but it was the gateway through which he would escape.

The deep ravine that contained the river tunnelled its way far up into a darkness that no starlight could penetrate and when the red pointers of camp-fires began to wink within it, they seemed far more brilliant than the dying fire beside which Harib and Eland lay asleep. To the lion high up above the river, the camp fires signified men on either side and he grunted and stalked away towards the hills. One by one the fires died, leaving only a twinkling of silent stars to watch for morning and a small wind from the sea to sigh for it and the lion to wait for it with grumbling impatience.

Grey light and the cackling of a black korhaan woke them and they blew up a fire from the still glowing embers of a root bound stump. They were warming their hands and watching their strips of rock rabbit meat sizzle when Harib uttered a sharp hiss of alarm and pointed with his chin towards the skyline, his hands reaching for his weapons.

Eland, hearing a sound behind him, turned and then called sharply to Harib: 'Wait, there are many.'

A quick count showed that they were surrounded by at least twenty bowmen; grey shapes advancing slowly,

156

the only sound a soft slithering and now and then a click of stone. Harib looked about him with wide angry eyes.

'You are right, there are too many,' he said, relaxing his grip on the bow. 'We can only speak.'

'I will speak,' Eland said. His eyes were hidden in darkness, but his words came clipped and fast. To risk losing now all he had dared to hope for in the last few days filled him with an almost uncontrollable anger against this chance, looming threat. He filled his lungs and shouted into the stillness and whiteness of spreading day. 'Put down your weapons. We will not fight with you.' His words rang clear over the stony veld and from somewhere behind him the black korhaan and his mate climbed into the air with their clattering, raucous cries.

'We have nothing,' he shouted again, and Harib, watching, saw that the band of advancing warriors had stopped.

'I think they are Oringa's tribe,' Harib said softly, and Eland shouted:

'Tell your king Oringa we know him; we can help him with the sourijs. He knows that if he harms us the sourijs will be angry.'

There was no movement for a while, then a little knot of the men drew itself together. One of them held up his hand as a signal for those behind and Harib expelled his breath in a release of tension.

'Are you red beard sourij?' a voice called across the grey stunted bush.

'I am he,' Eland said, 'and this is Outanqua Harib.'

'Where are you going to?' the voice came again.

'We journey to the stone house of the sourij chief,' Eland called back. Again there was an undecided movement as the band gathered. Light was beginning to flush the hills with a hint of sun and the soft grey green and yellow of the bushes was waxing into colour.

'We will come and speak with you,' the voice called at last and as they watched the band of armed men began to move towards them. The men were Oringa's, as they had guessed, and they surrounded Eland and Harib in a mild, almost amused anticipation, as though gathering for a spectacle. Harib sensed danger and in a casual way squatted by the fire and clicked his tongue in annoyance at the sight of the spoiled meat. There was some jostling and hissed discussion and the spokesman came a pace forward.

'If you touch your weapons we will kill you,' he said, then turned and once more there was a mumble of low talk. Eland, also feigning nonchalance, smiled at the men who watched him and, raising his arms slowly over his head, he stretched as though he had slept well, but he knew how his great muscles would ripple and bulge in the wakening sunlight and how his beard and hair would gleam like some sun god's from the far horizon. The men watched and whispered to one another.

The warriors' dress showed that they were ready for hunting or battle. Around their upper arms and above and below each knee were rings of sinew and some of ivory, but apart from their loin flaps they were naked. They carried bows, quivers of arrows, spears and varying sizes and types of carrier bags over their shoulders. Some had strings of red and black seeds and rock rabbit teeth around their necks and on their heads. They were were proportioned and well muscled, glistening with grease, but there was not one among them who weighed half as much as Eland.

Harib caught Eland's eyes and Eland moved very

slowly to join him squatting by the fire. They knew that their lives hung in the balance and in measuring the distance to their weapons they were silently resolving that if death was the verdict they would die fighting. Faintly now they began to hear a bellowing of cattle from over the low hills.

'They have cattle,' Harib said, quickly cocking his head. 'Perhaps they also journey to the stone house.'

Only their wits could save them now and any shred of a straw they could turn to advantage they must seize. Harib said loudly, 'If you take cattle to the stone house to trade with the sourijs who will speak for you? The sourijs are clever and will rob you if you do not know how to speak to them. Perhaps they will even turn their fire weapons against you and kill you and take your cattle away.' He paused. 'If you take us with you we will speak for you. This sourij,' he inclined his head towards Eland, 'will speak well for you with the sourij king. He can make you rich.'

There was no doubt that Harib's observations had made an impression and presently the group seemed to come to a decision. The spokesman beckoned peremptorily and told them to come, and Harib and Eland, careful to show arrogant indifference, gathered their weapons and few possessions and started towards the brow of the hill. The silent warriors with their ready bows moved with them on either side.

From the top of the hill they looked down in amazement over a gigantic herd of cattle; flanking the herd on all sides were herdsmen, and the smoke of their fires stretched far away into the distance of the valley basin. Immediately below them was a circle of grass huts with its clutter of people and their dogs and cooking fires.

This was certainly the camp of a main branch of the Hesaqua tribe and the thousands of head of cattle which grazed peacefully about it were undoubtedly stolen, the result of many successful raids. Oringa was indeed a robber chieftain and these were rich pickings, worth killing for, worth protecting. Both Eland and Harib knew that in the cattle lay either their destruction or their salvation and the slim lead which Harib had seized so quickly had given them the clue; if they could be of use to the Hesaquas in preserving or helping to trade the stolen herds, they would live; if not then they must surely die. As they walked down through the tough rhinoceros bush scrub and over baked boulders already touched by the sun, Eland saw another glimmer of hope. There was a chance that they still had his musket and it was almost certain that they did not know how to use it. If in the musket the Hesaquas could see a protection for the cattle, then this would be an additional point in their favour.

Once at the kraal of huts they were surrounded by women and children and shrilly barking dogs. They stood close together unmoving and when the sound had begun to die down Eland quite casually with hands on hips began to walk a slow circle and as he did so, the crowd fell back. He was an impressive figure there in the dusty camp, brick brown, broad-shouldered, long legs swinging slowly; even the armed men fell back and as he passed he gently pushed weapons down until he stood alone in the centre of the circle he had so magically cleared.

Now, with all the oratory of the Outanquas and with absolute mastery of the language, he spoke to them. With long rolling sentences and gestures of his body he told them stories of ships and cannons, of men on horseback, of food and drink that flowed in never ending bounty from the lands across the sea. He told them of the riches of beads and copper and tobacco that could be theirs, of how for ever afterwards, with the power of the fire weapons used for them by their sourij friends against all others, they could be masters of all the tribes in the land. Each man would be a chief, each man would be rich and powerful. All of this they could have if he and Harib were to help them. 'And now,' he said ending, 'I will speak with Oringa.'

For a long while no one moved, even the children seemed overawed by the strange figure who stood so imperiously before them. They peered from behind their naked mothers like rock rabbits from their holes. At last the spokesman gathered a group about him and moved away to sit before one of the huts. Harib and Eland could only glance at each other and wait. The palaver continued in slow motion over by the empty hut while the two prisoners watched under the silent scrutiny of their fascinated audience.

They made a half-hearted attempt at conversation and it no longer seemed strange to Eland that he should be chatting idly while his fate was being decided in the brains of savage robbers. But the dreams of snow and tinkling sleigh-bells and the rustling movements of a woman's dress were gone. All he desired, all he could dream of as good, would be to live and to sit in the sun and perhaps eat a sliver of meat and to drink a bowl of milk in the dust of the camp with the dogs and the children and the naked women. He did not know how close he was to the point of breaking, how worn the armour of his resistance or how slender the threads of sanity. He knew only that his anger had given way to an overwhelming sadness and when he looked away towards the mountains there seemed to be film of mist in his eyes.

The men were coming back. The spokesman stood before them and said gruffly, 'You can come with us,' and that was all. Harib heard Eland's breath like a deep sob, but he could not see his face for he had turned away. They had wondered why Oringa was not in evidence and Harib asked about him. 'Oringa is dead,' the spokesman said and walked away. Harib's eyes widened but he asked no more questions.

All that morning Eland and Harib remained unobtrusively in the background as the Hesaquas broke camp. The hut mats were rolled up, the frames were tied in bundles, the few wooden bowls and clay pots collected and all tied with leather thongs to the backs of pack oxen. When the sun was high the cavalcade swung slowly into motion, and after a while dust rose in a red pall that darkened the sun as the pace quickened. The bellowing and lowing of cattle drowned the whooping and whistling of herdsmen. Dogs barked and worked for their masters and the cattle moved forward answering to the secret commands that centuries had bred into their swinging heads.

Eland had found his musket and it had not been fired. Trotting behind the pack oxen, he and Harib found themselves almost alone with the women and children, for the able-bodied men of the tribe were herding and there was time for nothing else. In the evening they made camp and the cattle guards slept by their lonely fires and the women and children rolled themselves in their skins and slept under the sky. They had grazed the land behind them hard for a number of days and now they were racing towards the rich plains by the flat mountain in the country of the Cape men, through wastelands where no large herd could fatten.

With the dawn they were off once more at the same wild pace; eating and trampling the land before them like a swarm of locusts and the game herds thundered away on either side and all day long came the wailing and whistling and bellowing and the drumming thunder of hooves. And at night there was time only for sleep. On the third day the old mountains of the sea were before them and by the fifth the cattle were ranged in all their magnificence of numbers along the green slopes where clear water ran. Now the Hesaquas erected their huts and lay like drones in the sun. They smoked their dagga and made love to their women and drank thick milk spiced with whatever thing that crept or crawled. The fort lay no more than half a day's journey beyond and the smell of the cold western sea was a tingling exciting thing to Eland and Harib. Now at night they burned with impatience each in his own way, for the Hesaquas were no longer in a hurry. The cattle were safe, let them fatten. Meanwhile they had all they wanted and this was the time of the full moon, a time to sing and dance in a frenzy of dagga smoke, a time for story-telling, a time for pleasure. Tomorrow the sourijs would still be there and if not what did it matter? They were rich in cattle and tomorrow was of no consequence.

Eland and Harib lay on their backs on a pile of skins in their hut and the light of a full moon flowed in over them, touching the fleeces with silver and the antelope skins with gold. Their riches lay far behind them in a forgotten forest in a forgotten land. Could the streams still run there uncaring? And yet, here were over five thousand head of cattle. They would come in triumph. Tomorrow Eland would go alone to the fort. It had been decided by a council of warriors. Already the fort was whispering with rumoured news that the Hesaquas were close by with thousands of cattle and that there was a white man with them. A band of Cape men had told them and they had also told them that a war had begun again. Eland was to go alone and Harib would stay as a hostage.

'When the trading has been arranged, you must come to the fort,' Eland said again to Harib. 'Many rewards will await you there.' There was a moment of silence. 'What is there more I can do for you?'

Harib laughed softly. 'There is a girl,' he said. 'The one who speaks, they call her Tassie. If you will see her give her this. Ask her to come to me.' Harib held out the little glistening pendulum, aswing in the moonlight, a flash of gold.

Eland took it. 'This I promise you,' he said. 'On this above all else you have my word as a blood brother. This I will do gladly.'

They talked long into the night of the days that were gone away behind them. Like a final requiem for dead men, they talked of each one who had died and the blue glittering mountain above them rang with the sound of full moon. In turn they would drop small memories into the pool of reflection and the ripples of their remembering would flood the hut until silence came again. At last they slept, for all had been said.

In the morning Eland went away with the battered musket over his shoulder. At the top of a little rise he turned and waved and Harib waved back, then he was gone. For a while Harib stood watching the place where he had been and when he turned away his heart seemed to move with pain inside him. He busied himself as best he could during the day and by evening he was glancing over his shoulder at the path on the hill where the girl must come—if she came. But the hill path remained empty and that night he tortured himself and slept little; how long was it since he had known her? Was she still alive? Had she gone away to another man? He became heavy with despondency. It was stupid of him to hope and think so much. He must forget; there were plenty of other women. And then again he would see her and hear her laughter and see the flash of her teeth when she smiled and the swing of her hips. He saw children. He saw a new life in the haze of waking and sleeping. All day he thought of her and hoped still, but she did not come.

And then, when it was nearly evening, he saw her; he saw the tiny figure dwarfed by the mountain, and nearer, enveloped in the green lushness of the valley. And nearer, he was almost certain; he began to walk and then to run. The wind was cool on his cheek; she was coming to him. Tears of happiness squeezed from the corners of his eyes and the winter sun, blazing its way down into the sea, filled all the valley and the mountain slopes and the air itself with a lustre like gold.